G000123583

FALLING FOR GODS

THEIR DARK VALKYRIE #3

EVA CHASE

INK SPARK PRESS

Falling for Gods

Book 3 in the Their Dark Valkyrie series

All rights reserved. This book or any portion thereof may not be reproduced or used in any manner without the express written permission of the author, except for the use of brief quotations in a book review.

This is a work of fiction. Any resemblance to actual persons, living or dead, or actual events is purely coincidental.

First Digital Edition, 2018

Copyright © 2018 Eva Chase

Cover design: Rebecca Frank

Ebook ISBN: 978-1-989096-20-8

Paperback ISBN: 978-1-989096-21-5

 Created with Vellum

1

Aria

It was a little unsettling how distant the world of humans felt to me as I soared over the highway-split landscape. That world, the realm I was starting to think of as Midgard, had been my home for the twenty-two years I'd *been* a human. It'd been the only world I'd had any clue existed.

But anyone could have told you that I wasn't human anymore. The gigantic silver-white wings sprouting from my back were a pretty big tip-off. Also, the fact that I was flying through the air accompanied by five divine figures who'd never been human at all, who were coasting along in whichever way their godly magic allowed.

A month ago, I'd have been hustling through Philly's streets making a delivery for the gang that had most recently hired my courier services. Today I was on my way to seal a supernatural gateway that dark elves had been using to carry out horrible deeds on behalf of an evil giant.

All in a day's work for Asgard's only current valkyrie.

Even this high up, the summer wind was warm as it rippled over my wings and flicked a few strands of my rumpled blond hair across my cheek. The sun lit the fields below with a fierce glow and filled the air with the smell of baking grass. A trickle of sweat ran down the back of my neck. We'd decided to tackle the gate at midday because the dark elves, used to their dim caves in their own realm, weren't super keen on sunlight. At the moment, I wasn't feeling super keen on it myself.

The sights and smells of my former home sent my thoughts in other directions. What would Petey be up to today? Were his foster parents getting him out to the park or the swimming pool so he could enjoy the summer like he'd rarely gotten to under our mom's roof? Or maybe he was in school. I'd kind of lost track of the days of the week since the whole dying and valkyrie resurrection thing.

This was the first time I'd been back in Midgard since I'd left my little brother behind in the hopefully safe-keeping of his new foster family. The dark elves had threatened to kill him if I'd kept helping the gods around me. The elves had been killing people for who knew how long, dragging them off to the realm of fire where the giant Surt was transforming their bodies into draugr—ghoulishly bloated zombies.

My hands clenched at the memory of the bodies I'd seen in their caves, of the one elf's laughter when she'd talked about hurting Petey. If they laid one finger on him,

I'd wring all of their stumpy little necks without a hint of regret.

Hod, the god of darkness, turned his dark green eyes toward me from where he was gliding along on a patch of shadow like some kind of bizarre flying carpet. He couldn't actually see me with his blind gaze, but it mustn't have been too hard for him to guess what I might be thinking about on our return to this place.

"The elves have no idea where your brother is now," he said. "And they haven't been taking children—kids wouldn't be much use for Surt's army."

"Small mercies," I muttered, but a twinge of emotion ran through my chest at his attempted reassurance. It wasn't like me to want to lean on anybody, but Hod had managed to uncover a softer side I hadn't realized I even had—one that left me in tears at inopportune moments, and one that now and then gave me the urge to hide away in his embrace. Maybe that wasn't so surprising when he'd been so clear about how deep his affections for me ran.

That thought sent a different sort of shiver through me, one both giddy and nervous. This wasn't a good time for me to get soft. We were embarking on the next phase of a realm-crossing war.

"We could always take a little detour on the way home," Loki said in his usual wry voice, shooting me a grin. The trickster was striding along on his enchanted shoes of flight, the wind whipping his light red hair back from his pale face like the flames he could summon with a snap of his fingers.

Would it be easier seeing Petey without being able to

talk to him, to touch him, or simply holding on to my memories? Just a few days ago I'd come face to face with an illusion of him that had flinched away from me. It'd only been imaginary, a construct meant to break my will in the prison we'd found ourselves trapped in, but the moment had wrenched at me anyway.

My little brother was safer if I kept my distance. "When all the gates are sealed," I said. "When the dark elves can't get to him anymore."

"If you ever change your mind..." Loki said with a sweeping gesture. His amber eyes shone brighter. "This should be an interesting errand, in any case. It's difficult to believe that in all my time across the realms, I've never attempted to close off a gate between them."

"We made it through the gate easily enough before," Thor said, swinging the magical hammer he already had in his grasp. The brawny thunder god tipped his head to the fourth god with us: Hod's twin Baldur, light to the other's darkness. "One blast of Baldur's powers should send any guards who braved the sun running."

The bright god smiled, looking more assured and less dreamy than he'd been most of the time I'd known him. "I'll clear the way." His tone sounded more present too. I'd been with him through some painful moments in the prison Odin's raven of memory had constructed, reliving the chilling void of his death, but he seemed to have come out of that torment stronger. More determined to face the horrors that might still lie ahead of us.

Almost from the start, I'd been drawn to all four of the gods who'd combined their powers to bring me back from the dead in valkyrie form. But I couldn't deny that this more confident Baldur made my pulse kick up even faster than before.

"Let's not assume this will be easy, boys," Freya said with an imperious flap of her falcon cloak. The goddess of love and war peered toward the horizon, a fierce light glowing from her beautiful face. The golden waves of her hair glittered like an exquisite battle helm. Then she winked at me. "As usual, I expect the two of us have to keep this bunch on track."

Thor gave a bellow of a laugh, tossing his hammer from one hand to the other as if it weighed nothing at all. "The cave-dwellers should be very familiar with Mjolnir by now. They'll run. Just watch."

His warm brown gaze slid to mine with a gentler smile that felt as if it were meant just for me. It brought back the heat of his tender caresses when we'd come together in epic fashion not that long ago. I couldn't help grinning back.

We might have a war ahead of us, but we were ready for it. Closing this gate was the first step toward seeing Petey safe for good and preventing the invasion Surt was planning. He and his army could forget about taking even one piece of my former realm—or the new home I'd started to find in Asgard, the realm of the gods.

The landscape below us was becoming uncomfortably familiar. The gate we planned to shut was the one where we'd fought a battle with the dark elves last week—a battle in which we'd thought we were retrieving Odin from their clutches but instead had been led by a false version of him into that prison of memories. In those caves, I'd taken more lives with the dark power inside me, the one that valkyries had used to decide the fates of those on battlefields ages ago, than I'd have ever thought I'd be capable of.

They'd threatened my little brother. They'd killed who knew how many people for their master's army. I wasn't backing down until they were stopped for good.

The sagging wooden buildings around the gate looked even more decrepit than before. A handful of short dark-haired figures stood in a circle amid a patch of trees on the rocky hill at the edge of the ghost town. The oily energy the dark elves gave off made me shudder even from this distance.

Baldur raised his hands without waiting for an order. Light streamed from his skin and twined around his forearms and fingers. His gaze intent, he whipped the blaze forward.

With a high-pitched quavering, the wave of light crashed over the town and the gate beyond it. The guards around the gate toppled, their eyes searing pure black. No other figures stirred amid the buildings.

"Let's go, let's go," Loki said with a clap of his hands. He leapt down toward the trees. I swooped after him. The thick crack in the hillside came into view, like a black scar between the rocks and roots. That slick but sluggish energy wafted out of the gate from the realm it led into.

But we weren't looking to pay a visit this time. We wanted to make sure no one did, in either direction, ever again.

"See if you can work on it with those powers of

yours," Loki said with a flippant gesture toward Hod. "The gate stinks of darkness."

Hod shot him a grimace, but only a faint one. They'd come to some kind of broader truce since our paths had tangled on our way through Muninn's prison.

The dark god leaned over to test his palms against the opening. The power he'd given me as part of my resurrection reverberated in time with the energy emanating from the gate.

"There's magic woven across it, but I don't think I can use that to completely cut them off," Hod said. "They're creatures of darkness too. A clot of shadow isn't going to stop them for long."

"Can we close it physically?" I asked. "Does it have to be magic? Why not just plug it up with a bunch of these rocks?" I nodded to the hillside.

Loki tapped his lips. "I think they'd need to be magically fused into place to be sure of holding, but that's still a start. Oh, Thunderer, how about lending a little of your storminess to the proceedings? A thunderclap should do nicely to reorganize the landscape in a fitting fashion."

Thor heaved back his arm to hurl his hammer at the rocky terrain above the gate.

Before he could let it fly, a surge of bodies burst from the opening.

Dozens of dark elves charged toward us, faster than I'd have thought those stocky legs could have carried anyone. Spears and swords flashed in their hands. Thor let out a roar and whipped his hammer forward anyway, right at the mass of our attackers.

Several of the dark elves fell, bashed aside by Mjolnir, but the ones on either side of its path sprang at us unfazed. A wavering orange light danced along the blades of their weapons. I tried to wrench one from the hands of a man who lunged at me, and it seared a throbbing line across my palm. I yelped, yanking myself away and into the air with my wings.

"They've got magic on their weapons," I shouted. Magic they'd never had when we'd fought them before—a fiery magic that reminded me of Surt's realm. Had he offered them extra power to battle us with?

It wasn't going to save them. The other gods had drawn back as I had, but only to momentarily regroup. Thor's hammer flew back into his grasp. A burst of fire flared in Loki's hands. Hod's shadows whirled up around him. In that instant, I could taste all of it: the crackle of lightning and the hiss of fire, the warble of the dark and the keening of the light, all rushing through me together. I snapped my switchblade open in my hand.

We lashed out in the same moment. As I hurtled forward, my breath rushed out alongside the gods'—and their powers blasted into the swarm of dark elves like a series of earth-shaking fireworks. Shadow and fire merged into a dark wash of flame that consumed several bodies in its path. With a boom, light splintered into a hundred lightning bolts, dropping every dark elf they touched. In an instant, nothing was left of our enemies except bodies strewn around the gate. There wasn't even one left for me to claim with my blade and my valkyrie pull.

I jerked to a stop, hovering just over the gate with a sweep of my wings. My heart skipped a beat. That merging of the gods' powers had happened before, hadn't it? When we'd rushed in to save the real Odin from Surt's cage. The fighting then had been so quick and brutal I hadn't stopped to think about it at the time, but I couldn't ignore it now. Something was going on, something that hadn't happened the first few times I'd fought beside the gods.

What the hell did it mean? And more importantly, could we use it again if we wanted to, to kick every dark elf ass to Kingdom Come?

2

Baldur

A rush of electricity sang through my veins as my hurled light melded around Thor's hammer. With a shriek, it exploded into a hail of lightning.

I glanced at my older brother, and he grinned back at me with his eyebrows raised. Neither of us knew what had just happened, but it had repelled the dark elves, so the "what" didn't really matter just yet.

"Wasn't that interesting?" Loki said, studying his hands. Before we could have a real conversation about that strange merging of our powers, another swarm of attackers burst from the gate.

Aria let out a cry and sprang forward. My pulse stuttered in fear for her as I leapt into the fray with the others. But our valkyrie could hold her own. A splinter of lightning sparked from the tip of her switchblade, and her other hand brushed one elf's forehead, yanking the life from him with her valkyrie powers.

The echo of my fellow gods' movements washed over me as I moved in turn. It wasn't just our magic that appeared to have merged. Without even trying, I found myself heaving forward a burst of power alongside Loki, Hod, and Thor, all of us together. Ari spun around with another slash of her knife at the same moment.

All the energy we cast out twined together and ripped through the charge of dark elves. Fiery light, shadowy sizzling bolts, and a flaming crash of thunder sent their bodies flying. Freya rushed in with a slash of her sword, but there was barely anyone left to duel.

A rush of exhilaration tickled up from my chest. I might not know what was happening, but it was clear we were connecting in some way we never had before. My brothers and the trickster were as invested in this fight as I was, and we would win it together.

A few of the elves managed to dodge to the side quickly enough to escape our magic. I lunged after one—and through the light shimmering in and around my body, a cold tendril unfurled. A dark icy finger like a strip of the void that had enclosed me in death, both centuries ago and just a few days ago in Muninn's prison. It snaked around my stomach.

My chest clenched, and my jaw tightened. I slammed my fist into the dark elf's head with an extra smash of light. The shiver of darkness inside me tugged at my gut, and I smacked him again, sending him reeling into a tree.

My lips twitched as he groaned. Yes, let him suffer a little before he died, after everything his people had—

I caught myself, snapping my fingers shut just a second shy of searing his skin with light that would have wounded but not ended his misery. A sharper rush of cold flooded me.

What was I doing? What was I *thinking*? Torturing this man wouldn't be justice.

I ended his life with a quick blast of light to his forehead, searing through his mind. My legs felt steady enough as I turned back to the others, but that slip of shadow had coiled even more insistently around my gut.

The void had crept into me while I'd floated there in that endless chilling nothingness. I'd felt it crawl down my throat and seep through my skin. Had some of it stayed with me when I'd come back into the light? I'd spent so long avoiding even thinking about my death and the torment that had come with it, I'd never looked inside myself for it all that closely. Perhaps it had been there all along, without the chance to awaken.

This might be the first battle I'd fought where I was fully present in over a thousand years.

The other dark elves around us had all fallen. Loki strode up to the ragged opening of the gate.

"Let's close this up before yet another assault comes our way," the trickster said. "All of our powers together should do the trick nicely, I'm starting to think."

I lifted my arms, summoning the glow coursing through my limbs back into my hands. Thor struck the rocks above the crevice with his hammer. They crackled and jittered with lightning as they tumbled across the opening.

Before they could fall through into the blackness

beyond, Loki cast a wave of fire over them. Instinctively, I tossed a burst of light to meet his flames. Our combined powers fused the rocks between them and melted them into the edges of the crevice.

Hod released a flood of shadow over the molten mass, cooling it into a solid barrier that sealed the gate from top to bottom. The surface shone like obsidian.

Aria prodded the seal with her switchblade. The glossy mass resisted even the jab of the blade, not a scratch forming beneath it. Freya came up beside us and prodded the spot with a whirl of her magic as well.

She stepped back with a satisfied expression. "That feels as though it'll hold. Now what in Hel's name was happening between the rest of you?"

"I don't know," Hod said. "The last couple of times we've fought together, I've felt a sort of synchronicity—as if our movements and powers are flowing toward each other. I've never seen my shadows combine with anyone else's magic before."

"I can feel it too," Aria said. "Like a hum between all of us."

"Between you and the four of them," Freya said. "I haven't felt anything different."

The valkyrie nodded, her gray eyes sliding over us. "You didn't lend your powers to making me, right?" she said to the goddess. "They were the ones who summoned me. I'm a patchwork valkyrie made out of the pieces of your powers. Maybe that's got something to do with it?"

"It has to," Thor put in. "Odin may have a clearer idea. We can see what he makes of it."

He made a motion for us to take to the sky again. My

body balked for a second before I called up the beam of light that would carry me onward.

The Allfather had stayed back, rather than join us on this mission, to continue recovering from his long imprisonment. We hadn't wanted to delay our efforts to contain the dark elves. Of course he'd want to hear our report and all that had happened. And well he should, as our leader. But I found I wasn't looking forward to that meeting at all.

———

You wouldn't have known Odin was at anything other than his best to see him now, poised on his throne in the meeting room of his great hall. He sat tall, his silvered brown beard trimmed down from its previous wild state, his single dark eye alert. His great gleaming spear leaned against the arm of the throne, ready, as if he might need to leap into battle in an instant.

The ruler of Asgard didn't believe in showing weakness.

"This effect you saw," he said, his penetrating gaze roving over each of the six of us in turn. "You've never experienced anything like that before?"

"Only today and briefly in the fight when we found you in Muspelheim," Thor said.

"It appears to be connected to our valkyrie," Loki said, resting a hand that looked unusually tentative on Aria's shoulder. "Or rather, that we have become increasingly connected through her. The process of summoning a valkyrie—each of us contributing some of our essence—it took a lot of out us, and most of what it took went into reforming her spirit as she is now. My best guess is that when she's fighting alongside us, something of that merging activates and allows our powers to work in greater harmony."

Harmony. Yes. That was the word for what I'd felt in those moments as we'd pushed back the dark elves together. I'd spent most of my existence striving for harmony, but I'd never had it come to me as deeply and fully as then. I'd found it thanks to Aria.

Her eyes caught mine from across the semi-circle we'd formed in the high-ceilinged room, and she shot me a little smile as if she were thinking the same thing. And I realized what I'd just thought wasn't entirely true. I'd experienced that exquisite harmony one other time— when Loki, Thor, and I had come together to demonstrate our desire for our valkyrie in every way we could.

A trickle of heat coursed over my skin. I'd much rather find the sensation again there than on the battlefield, given the choice.

"Aria isn't the first valkyrie you summoned," Odin said. "Did you see a similar effect with the ones previous?"

"The others... didn't remain with us for long enough for any connection to really gel," Hod said.

"We've been through much more with Ari," Thor said. "The bond between us—it goes beyond the hand we had in creating her new life." He cleared his throat, as if he weren't sure how much detail to go into there. "We've come to understand each other on every level: mentally, emotionally..."

Physically. The slight arch of the Allfather's eyebrow made me suspect that he'd guessed that aspect even if no one had outright told him. Very little escaped Odin. I couldn't read from his expression how he might feel about the idea that three of his sons and his brother by blood-oath might be centering their affections on the same non-godly woman.

Then Odin's gaze found me. "You haven't said much about the situation, my son," he said. "Do your impressions align with the others?"

"Yes," I said quickly. "The sense of harmony, the bond that's been forming—I'm sure it's all related." I paused, unsure how to continue. The mechanics of magic were far from my forte. And ever since Odin had returned to us, I'd found it hard to look him in the eye for very long and still remember how to use my tongue.

I'd have given anything to bring my father back to Asgard. A large part of me was overjoyed at our victory, ecstatic to see him sharp and determined as ever in his throne. We had been aimless for a long time without his guiding force, and now, with Surt preparing to invade both Asgard and Midgard, we needed that guidance more than ever.

But no matter how bright my happiness might be, a shadow lurked beneath it. I couldn't erase the memories Loki had shown us from my head—and I shouldn't want to.

My father had approved of my murder. He might even have encouraged it. He'd let me fall into the vast void that had wrenched me apart so thoroughly I couldn't imagine my spirit would ever heal completely, as part of some immense plan he'd never bothered to speak to me about, before or after.

No, he'd let me think any blame I could have assigned belonged with my twin, who had thrown the mistletoe spear that had struck me down, and Loki, who'd guided Hod's hand. Where was the justice in *that*?

I hadn't spoken to Odin of it. He'd been recovering, and I wasn't certain Loki would even want me to reveal the secret he'd betrayed. But most of all, I hadn't known what to say that would express the tangled emotions inside me, or what Odin could possibly offer me in return that would tease them apart into some sort of peace.

As the Allfather turned back to the others, the tendril of darkness that had tugged at me earlier twisted around my gut and shot through the muscles of my legs. Before I could contain it, my heel jammed against the floor. A small crack spread across the smooth stone surface, spidering at its edges.

My heart lurched. I eased to the side, covering the mark with my foot. No one was looking at me. No one had seemed to notice.

I'd held the darkness inside me at bay for all those years by burying myself in a dreamy haze. I couldn't go back to that. I'd just have to quash it down with all the light I had in me. I'd survived this long. A sliver of the void couldn't overpower me.

"This is a new development, but a welcome one," Odin was saying. "Combining your powers around the valkyrie may be the key to defeating Surt quickly and decisively. We haven't located any of the other gates to Nidavellir yet, have we? Any spare time you have until we do, you should practice together, experiment. The more you can control this new skill, the more potent it will be."

A pleased smile slipped across his lips with those last words. The master planner had discovered a new strategy. I should have been happy too, but an uneasy shiver traveled through me.

3

Aria

Odin leaned back in his tall chair with a satisfied expression, as if he'd said everything he needed to and now we were all supposed to jump to do his bidding. His presumptuous attitude itched at me.

Who the hell was he to call all the shots here anyway? Okay, sure, the king of the gods, but he'd been stuck in some cage locked away from the rest of the world for decades. He hardly even knew that much about what had been happening around his capture, let alone anywhere else. The six of us had been working together—and working well—for weeks now. He'd only just joined the party.

And he hadn't bothered to ask *my* opinion about any of this.

"We can't count only on this special power, whatever exactly it is, right?" I said. "We have to find out exactly what Surt is doing right now, what plans he's making, so we can go in prepared."

Odin's one-eyed gaze settled on me with prickling intensity. It was hard to focus completely on that eye and not also the knot of scar where his other one had once been.

"I am keeping watch over Muspelheim from my high seat," he said.

"Great," I said. "Then you know how big this army of his is already? You've heard him talking about when he thinks he'll attack?"

The Allfather's mouth tightened. I got the impression he didn't appreciate getting this many questions thrown at him.

"The suggestion that my high seat allows me to 'see all' has been slightly overstated," he said. "I can look down over anywhere I please, but walls still restrict my view. Surt has kept his strategizing and his army mostly shut away."

As if I trusted this guy to tell us the full story even if he'd seen something useful. I set my hands on my hips. "We've got to get down there and take a closer look, then, don't we?" Get behind those walls if we could. Make sure there weren't things Odin was deciding not to tell us.

"Scouting out Muspelheim will not be an easy task. Surt has shut away the gates that allow access to all the other realms inside his fortress. Getting there is simple enough, but anyone who does would have to fight their way out."

"You've got your rainbow bridge magic for an instant transport out."

Odin chuckled at my phrasing, but his gaze didn't lighten. "Bifrost is a powerful tool, but not a subtle one. Surt would have his guards on anyone who used it the moment it appeared."

Okay, fair enough. But I'd make my way back to Asgard before without any bridge or gateway. That was the whole reason the gods had summoned a valkyrie to help them find Odin.

"*I* can go," I said. "My connection to Valhalla means I can will myself back there if I need to, no matter where I am. I've done it before."

Loki grinned. "That's the spirit. You'll be out-scheming us all soon enough, pixie."

Odin's expression shifted, a curious light coming into his eyes. Or maybe it was amused. I wasn't sure I liked it either way.

"An excellent point," he said. "All right then, my unexpected valkyrie. Are you proposing to set off on this scouting mission immediately?"

Across the room from me, Baldur was frowning. "She should get some rest first after the fighting today."

Odin's gaze didn't waver from me. I raised my chin. The question felt like a test—of how committed I was to this course of action, of whether I really had the guts to follow through. If I backed down even until tomorrow, I'd be giving the Allfather room to doubt me.

"I'm not that tired. I can make a quick initial sweep to give me an idea where I'd want to spend more time spying the next time around."

"I don't see how it could hurt anything," Freya said from where she'd come to stand beside her husband. She patted Odin's arm. "It *would* be good to have a clearer sense of our enemy."

Thor had turned to me, his forehead furrowed. "Are you sure this is a good idea, Ari? Surt will be watching for anyone from Asgard. It's been a long day already."

I shrugged, offering him a reassuring smile. "I'll sleep better tonight knowing what Surt and his minions are up to right now. If I start to get tired or I feel like I'm in danger, I'll just leap back to Valhalla. Nothing to worry about."

He gave me a look as if to say I should know he'd worry about me anyway, but his stance relaxed a smidge. "I'd feel better if I—or any of us—could go with you."

"That isn't possible though, right?"

Loki let out a huff of breath. "Sadly, it does sound as though the rest of us would be reliant on tangling with Surt directly to make our way home. Unfortunate, because I'd quite like a longer look for myself at that realm he's made his own. But I have every faith in your skills and judgment. If I can't go, you're my next choice out of all of us. I did lend you some of my wits, after all."

"I had plenty before you did any lending," I said, giving him a playful glower, and he laughed.

"Why do you think I picked you, pixie?"

Yes—I was Loki's valkyrie more than anyone else's. He was the one who'd insisted they try summoning a woman with a little more street smarts and a little less pureness of heart. If they'd stuck with the same criteria they'd used for their first three valkyries, my life would have ended with the impact of that idiot junkie's speeding jeep.

And the gods might never have found their way to Odin. I'd made that possible. I could make a difference here too. For them, and for Petey and everyone else Surt threatened.

"I can go by Yggdrasil, can't I?" I said, lifting my chin to indicate I was ready to get started. "I just need to know which branch to take."

Odin rose from his throne-like chair, gripping his silver spear like a walking stick. He'd left off his rumpled broad-brimmed hat, but somehow he looked even taller without it. He strode forward with his cloak rustling at his heels. "Come along then. I'll show you."

Loki brushed his fingers over my arm as I turned to follow the Allfather. Thor nodded to me, and Baldur aimed his bright smile my way. They drifted toward their own halls as we left Odin's, but Hod fell into step beside me.

"Did you think I needed an extra escort?" I asked the dark god with a raise of my eyebrow he couldn't see.

"I don't have anywhere better to be," he said casually. "Do you mind the company?"

Not when it was him, and not when my only other company was the ominous Odin. "I guess I can cope with a little hovering. As long as you're not planning on trying to convince me not to go."

Hod guffawed at that. "Oh, believe me, valkyrie, I know better than that by now."

It was only a short walk from Odin's hall down the marble-tiled path to the immense Valhalla, which once hundreds of reborn warriors and maybe as many valkyries had called home. We trailed along behind the

Allfather, who walked briskly without a backward glance. The sun shone bright but not as starkly as it had down in Midgard, the breeze pleasantly warm and full of sweet flowery scent. It might have been a nice little stroll if I hadn't known I was on my way to a realm of barren rock and flowing magma.

Hod hesitated for a moment inside the great hall with its rows of long tables and its walls hung with gleaming weaponry. I guessed he hadn't come into this place often enough to have a solid sense of the layout. Shadows unfurled around him, testing the edges of the benches, as we made our way more slowly to the golden throne at the far end.

Odin stopped at the huge stone-lined hearth beside that throne. The back of the hearth gave way to a deep void I'd stepped into once before, when I'd traced Odin's kidnapping to the realm of the dark elves. I wasn't sure which I'd have looked forward to seeing less: those cramped dank caves or the searing heat of Surt's realm.

At least in the realm of fire, I had room to really fly.

As Hod and I reached the hearth, he touched my shoulder. When I turned toward him, he raised his hand to my cheek, his blind gaze knowing exactly where to find my eyes now.

"Look after yourself," he said. "I'll wait here for you until you get back."

A lump rose in my throat. Was he thinking about my last venture through Valhalla, when I'd dragged myself back to the gods bleeding and beaten? "I plan on making it back on my feet this time," I said.

"I'm glad to hear it." He dipped his head, and I

bobbed on my toes to meet his kiss. His shadows wisped around me, holding me like an echo of his lean arms. In that moment, I wished I could just stay here with him and forget about Muspelheim and Surt and the rest—lose myself in the passion we'd sparked between us before.

Not just passion. He loved me. He'd told me so. That knowledge quivered in my chest, joyful and nervous at the same time. I wasn't sure I was equipped to properly handle my own heart yet, let alone anyone else's. But it felt like an honor to be given this much devotion from a man who'd endured so much.

I kissed him hard, wanting him to know how much even this gesture meant to me. Hod traced his thumb over my cheek and eased back, his pale cheeks faintly flushed. He kissed me once more on the forehead and sat down on the nearest bench to begin his vigil.

"Ready?" Odin said with just a hint of dryness. I had no idea what he thought of the intimacy he'd just seen, but I didn't really give a damn about his approval anyway. There didn't seem to be much point in hiding just how close all four of my gods and I had become.

"Let's go," I said, swiping my hands together.

The Allfather ducked into the cavern behind the fireplace, and I slipped after him. On the opposite side, the prone tree stretched out like a path of bark and branches into a thick nothingness.

The air was chillier here. A shiver crept over my bare arms as I padded after Odin along the trunk. With a twitch of my shoulders, I unfurled my wings from my back. If I knew one thing for sure, it was that I'd want to be prepared to fly the second I stepped through this gate.

"Why did you release all your warriors and valkyries anyway?" I asked, watching the sway of Odin's cloak ahead of me. "Baldur told me that you let them all leave a while ago. I guess there aren't even any of them left after all this time, wherever they went? But it'd be a lot easier with an army of our own."

Odin hummed to himself. "It was time to end that chapter," he said, as if that explained anything at all. He drew to a halt and pointed to a branch at his right. "That way will lead you to Muspelheim."

"Okay." I flexed my wings. "Any last-minute tips?"

I hadn't really expected any, but the Allfather gave me a foreboding look. "Stay wary. Move quickly. Don't let yourself become distracted from your task, or you may find you're the one caught."

All right then. All of that advice fell into the category of *No kidding*. I bobbed my head to him with a tense smile and started down the branch.

A cloying heat seeped from the patch of thicker darkness at its end with a whiff of sulfur. I braced myself and sprang through the gate.

I tumbled out into hot bitter-smelling air over a stretch of jagged rock. A cliff loomed near me, and a river of magma churned by several feet away, casting a reddish glow over the dark gray stone. A dim glimmer lit the dull sky, barely enough that you could call it sunlight.

With a flap of my wings, I whirled myself around— and caught sight of the dragon just opening its eyes where it was sprawled by the edge of the cliff. Its gaze turned toward me. Stone scales clinked as the creature lifted itself onto its taloned feet, its wings spreading with a warble of air.

I wasn't going to stick around to find out what that thing had in store for me. I took off toward the mountains on the other side of the river.

A searing gust of wind caught my feathers. I swooped into a crevice in the mountainside wide enough to fit me but not the dragon. A frustrated roar echoed through the air as it wheeled in the sky behind me.

I ventured along the crevice until it opened up around the side of the mountain. Peering out, I couldn't see any sign of the dragon nearby. With a triumphant grin, I scrambled out and soared onward.

I'd seen a pretty limited amount of Muspelheim during my last "visit." Just the cavern where Muninn had constructed her prison and the valley between it and the other cave where Surt's dark elf allies had locked away Odin. The realm around me appeared as vast as it was desolate. How was I going to find the giant?

When we'd been searching for the dark elves' gate before, I'd used the heightened senses the gods had given me to trace their oily energy. All living beings gave off some sort of tingling of life. It didn't look like there was much living anywhere here. If I found a whole bunch of people all together, that would probably be Surt's army. The other-than-undead part of it, anyway.

I reached out with my senses as I flew on, braced for any hint of those vibrations of life. A soft quavering touched me from somewhere to my right. I veered toward it, pushing my wings faster. Within a few minutes, the sensation had expanded into a faint ragged hum that grazed my skin.

A different feeling niggled at the back of my neck at the same time. I glanced behind me and then all around, but I didn't see anyone nearby. Maybe it was just my paranoia in this freaky place making me think someone— or something—must be watching me.

I glided over a groove in the landscape that looked like it might once have been an actual stream, now dried up. Farther along it, skeletal husks of trees that I suspected would have crumbled in a stiff breeze scattered its edge. The remains of some kind of forest? It was hard to believe any vegetation on that scale had ever grown here.

Not much could have grown here *now*, that was for sure. The heat squeezed tighter around me, my throat burning each time I took a deeper breath.

The hum of life ahead of me expanded. I soared over a stretch of jagged hills, and my gaze came to rest on an immense stone fortress on the other side of a great barren plain up ahead. Several wide towering buildings stood inside a wall that looked as if it'd been made by tossing boulders into place somewhat haphazardly. Magma flowed around those high but uneven walls like a pulsing glowing moat. Even as far away as I was, I could make out figures guarding the place from ledges along the wall and balconies on the jutting towers.

If that wasn't Surt's home, then I was the Queen of Portugal.

The nagging sense of being watching rippled down

my back again. I jerked around, hoping to take my pursuer by surprise.

Nothing stirred amid the hills except a strip of frayed cloth the sluggish breeze couldn't tug away from the thorny leafless shrub that had snagged it. I studied the landscape for a minute longer and then moved on.

Instead of heading straight for the fortress, which seemed incredibly unwise, I circled around and flew along the line of low cliffs to the east. As I drew closer, more and more guards came into view along the walls. Others were sparring in the fortress's courtyard. Figures moved past the rough windows in the stone-slab walls.

Not all of them were dark elves. Several were either too tall or too light-haired to be those. And then there were the spidery creatures crawling across the sides of the buildings. I shuddered, remembering the one that had nearly crushed me between its knobby legs a few days ago.

Surt had gathered an army, all right. I wouldn't have believed that many people could live in this whole realm, it was so bleak. And those figures didn't move like the shuffling draug I'd seen before.

Odin might be confident, but I wasn't so sure one special magic trick was going to be enough to bring this giant down.

I was just soaring closer, every sense perked, when a shadow swept over me. Another rock dragon was diving toward me from higher above. My nerves jumped, and I threw myself toward the shelter of the cliff.

There were no hiding places there, just sheer rock everywhere I looked. The dragon's talons raked the stone just inches from my shoulder with an ear-splitting screech. I yelped and reached out to Asgard, to the golden gleam of Valhalla.

The taste of stale mead ran over my tongue, and with a jolt, the bitter heat of Muspelheim fell away from me. I stumbled onto the worn floorboards of Valhalla. Hod was at my side, gripping my arm to steady me, before I could catch my balance myself.

"Are you all right?" he asked. "Did you discover anything?"

I rubbed the shoulder the dragon had nearly gouged. "Yes," I said. "And not anywhere near as much as I'd have liked to. If the seven of us are going to take down Surt's army, I think we're going to need a hell of a lot of training."

4

———

Aria

"Now!" Thor bellowed, and we all flung ourselves toward the targets. As my arm swung with my switchblade and my other hand shot out as if to wrench life from the wooden figure in front of me, four other pulses beat in unison with mine.

Loki's fire veered like the arc of my slash, streaming to speed Thor's hammer forward even faster. Bolts of light and shadow streaked around its trail and whipped apart again. Sparks and slivers of darkness exploded through the row of dummies. Before my feet had even touched the ground, our targets had crumpled into a heap of charred kindling. A thin smoky smell laced the warm air.

"Wow," I said, my chest heaving as I caught my breath. I wasn't just awed by the impact of our combined powers. Now that we were consciously trying to fight in unison, to bring out the connection that was growing between us, these merged attacks had come easier and easier. But with each practice strike, my awareness of the gods around me deepened. For a second or two, each time we hurled ourselves forward, it felt almost as if I was part of them and they were part of me.

Somehow that sensation was equally exhilarating and terrifying. I'd never felt so close to anyone in my life, not even my brothers. But in that moment, I wasn't just me anymore. If I let myself go even more than this, would I start to lose myself?

"One set left!" Freya called from the sidelines. She'd helped set up the targets in this field on the outskirts of the godly city. From the eager light in her midnight-blue eyes, I suspected she wished she could join in. Not that the goddess of war wasn't a formidable force without any mystical bonding going on.

The five of us stepped into a formation that was becoming automatic: me front and center, Loki and Thor to my left and right, Hod and Baldur just a step behind and between us. Thor raised his hammer, our signal to focus. We waited one beat to be sure we were all ready, and then we charged at our next set of targets.

I jabbed my switchblade into the straw chest of the dummy at the front with a satisfying crunch. A surge of energy washed over and through me as the gods hurled their magic forward. They were accomplishing a hell of a lot more than I was. For every one foe I might have been able to take down, their combined powers could have toppled fifty or more. But it didn't work if I wasn't fighting with them. We'd experimented with that.

When I'd stood on the sidelines with Freya and the four of them had tried to launch into battle in sync, their powers didn't just fail to intertwine. The sense that I was supposed to be out there with them had wrenched through me hard enough to make me stumble toward them, as if I'd been yanked.

Even now, as Thor chuckled at the ruin we'd left of the targets, that more intense awareness lingered. Baldur's contribution to my valkyrie transformation had been the ability to sense people's emotions— hopes and desires, regrets and guilt—which if I'd been a proper valkyrie I'd have used to decide which side on the battlefield deserved to win and who was worthy of being sent up to Valhalla on their death. I could read human beings pretty well, but the minds of the gods had been nearly impenetrable, even when I'd tried.

Now, though, as Loki shot me one of his sly grins, a jitter of restless tension reached me. And when Baldur's fingers grazed the small of my back in a brief but affectionate caress, along with the warm tingle of pleasure, a pang of distress echoed through me.

I turned to study the god of light. He smiled at me, his boyishly handsome face and shaggy white-blond hair as bright as ever. But that pang I'd just felt wasn't the only tremor of uneasiness that had reached me while I was near him this morning.

"Are you all right?" I asked, touching his arm.

Something flickered in Baldur's bright blue eyes, but his smile didn't falter. He took my hand in his with a gentle squeeze. "Never better," he said. "It's amazing how much more we all become when we can build off each other's power, isn't it?"

That wasn't really what I'd been asking him, but he did *sound* okay. Maybe that feeling of connection was unsettling him a little just like it was me, simply because it took some getting used to.

Loki brushed his hands together, scanning the mess we'd made with all the dummies we'd destroyed over the last few hours. "Odin will certainly be proud," he said. His wry voice had more of an edge to it than sounded completely comfortable.

The Allfather had requested that we take up this training, but he hadn't come out to observe any of it. Unless he was watching us from up in that high seat of his that apparently could give him a view over all of the nine realms. The thought made my skin crawl.

Who knew what he was doing while we were running around trying to prepare for war anyway? He'd told us what he wanted us to do, but not how he was going to fit into that strategy. He hadn't seemed all that concerned when I'd reported what I'd seen in Muspelheim, only nodded and gazed off in thought. He'd better not be planning to sit on his throne while we did all the fighting.

Of course, maybe not everyone here was looking forward to fighting next to Odin. It was hard not to think of the things Loki had shown us from his memories: the way the Allfather had used him as his villain and let him take on all the blame when Odin himself had ordered the trickster god to spread chaos in Asgard. The way Loki had pleaded in vain to be released from that duty. I didn't know how he'd managed to keep his peace with Odin for so long afterward, carrying that secret.

"It was good for us to practice," Hod said, swiping his hand through the sweat-damp fringe of his short black hair. "We'll fight together like this more effectively the more we've gotten used to the rhythm of it." *He* might have felt more at peace with Loki after those recent revelations, but I guessed it was going to take a while longer before he got out of the habit of arguing with the trickster on a regular basis.

"And it very effectively keeps us out of his hair, doesn't it?" Loki said in the same light but barbed tone.

Hod looked as if he were about to mutter something in return. I jumped in before he could.

"Are we ever going to talk to Odin about it?" I said. "About the things he asked Loki to do—about the fact that it seems like he *wanted* Ragnarok to happen? None of you knew about that before. We can't pretend it doesn't matter."

The five figures around me went stiff and silent in an instant. Thor rubbed his mouth. "We will speak with him about it. Of course we will. But now, with Surt posing such a huge threat—we have to stand together against him before we can sort things out between us in Asgard."

"He hasn't even been home for a week yet, after all that time imprisoned," Baldur added. "He'll be able to give us better answers when he's back to his usual self."

"It's going to be a hard conversation," Hod said. "It'll be better for *all* of us to have it when we don't have much more pressing troubles hanging over us. It's been centuries—a few more weeks can't hurt."

Loki's gaze had slid from one of the gods to the next as they'd given their excuses. His jaw tightened, his mouth twisting at a pained angle for just a second before he caught it but long enough to make my gut twist in response.

"You didn't seem to feel the past mattered so little just a few days ago, oh dark one," he said with a half-hearted smile, sounding only weary now. He shrugged. "And so it goes in Asgard."

Hod frowned at him. "I don't see *you* bringing it up with Odin."

"Because all the complaints I made before got me so far?" Loki waved him off. "He and I know where we stand with each other. If you're fine standing where you always have as well, that's your prerogative." He swiveled on his heel. "I meant to do some more scouting today. There must be at least a few more gateways between Nidavellir and Midgard. With a little luck, I'll track down another for us to seal."

"Hey." I caught his elbow before he could stalk away. The trickster paused and peered down at me, one eyebrow rising.

Loki knew how to put on his masks of indifference and carelessness so well, but I knew better than to believe this one. I'd seen firsthand what he'd endured to live here in Asgard, never accepted as an equal to the gods, never really trusted or respected. He'd accepted all that because of his blood-oath with Odin until he'd been pushed up to his breaking point, but even now, with the truth revealed, how much had changed for him?

I squeezed his arm. "I could come with you. We

found that first gate together." *I* was still with him, even if a valkyrie's support didn't count half as much as the other gods'.

Loki's smile softened, and I caught a little more of the turmoil behind his amber gaze. "The offer is appreciated, pixie," he said. "But I think after all this group bonding, me, myself, and I is plenty of company."

"Okay." What I'd said didn't feel like enough. I reached up to grasp his tunic, and he bent his tall slim form to give me the kiss I'd been angling for. His lips lingered against mine for just long enough to leave my heart beating faster and my nerves singing for more.

"Perhaps we can enjoy each other's company tonight," he said with a wink when he eased back, sounding more like his usual breezy self.

"I could possibly be convinced," I said, unable to contain my smile, and he strode off chuckling.

Thor took in the field with its heaps of splintered and seared wood and straw. "I suppose we'd better get on with cleaning up this mess."

"Oh, you can bash it all into dust in a matter of minutes, can't you, Thunderer?" Freya said. "Ari, let's see what else we have around, before you lot resort to demolishing our forests."

She motioned for me to follow her, so I fell into step beside her as she headed toward the city in the direction of her hall. She'd housed half of the warriors who'd been honored in Asgard way back when, and I guessed they'd needed lots to keep them busy. That first batch of targets we'd brought over from her storage rooms.

The goddess tucked a stray golden wave behind her

perfectly shaped ear. "I can't blame them, you know," she said. "For not knowing what to say to Odin? I'm not sure how to start to talk to him about the subject myself, and he's *my* husband. The way he perceives things, he may even have already gleaned the fact that we know."

"So why not just bring it up then?" I said. "*I* would, but, I mean, I wasn't even there when all that happened. I've got no idea about the details. It's not going to mean much coming from me. Do you think he's going to get angry?"

"I don't know. I think maybe..." She sighed. "There's a saying you mortals have about cans of worms? You bring up one thing and so many other concerns spring to the surface, and then you can't put any of them back. Odin rules Asgard. To challenge his judgment, the decisions he's made, it could rock the foundations of this place."

I kicked at a pebble lying on the tiled road we'd just stepped onto. "It seems to me those foundations are already pretty shaky. How do you build them up better if you pretend they're just fine?"

"It's more complicated than that," Freya said. "You *weren't* there. And there are so many things..."

She paused for long enough that I started to think we were done with the subject too. Then she said, "I have a daughter. Or maybe it's 'had' now. From my first marriage—Hnoss. After Ragnarok, when we were all reborn, she said to me that she thought Odin had more of a hand in events than he was letting on. She wanted me to ask him to—I don't know. Admit to us what his plans had been? Reassure us about the future? He and I had already been getting closer back then."

She dipped her head with a grimace. "I didn't believe her. I thought she was jealous of the closeness we'd developed, imagining the worst of him to excuse those hateful feelings. We argued so many times, and then she left. She couldn't stand to stay here while I stood by him. And she was right, this whole time. Maybe not in the anger she held toward him—that will depend on his reasons—but in her suspicions that I denied."

The regret in her voice made my stomach clench. If my mother had cared even a fraction that much about me or Petey...

"She must be in the nine realms somewhere, then, right?" I said. "We'll find her. You can talk to her, tell her you're sorry. It doesn't have to be complicated. You've got to at least try."

Freya nodded. "I do. I just wish I knew where to start."

"We'll find her," I said again, firmly, even though I didn't have the slightest clue how I was going to fulfill that promise.

5

Loki

I shuddered as I came out of the tunnel, sending a quick lick of flame over me to burn away any cobwebs and other debris that might have attached to my body as I'd searched the abandoned mine. The late afternoon sun blazing between the tree branches overhead and the crisply green smells of the forest were a welcome relief. How the dark elves managed not to go completely mad living in dank spaces like that their entire existence, I didn't know.

Of course, given the sorts of adventures they'd been getting up to lately, one might make the argument that they *had* gone mad.

I'd had high hopes for this old mine. It was only miles from the town where I'd spotted dark elf activity in the past, where Ari and I had noted the symbols the dirt-eaters appeared to be marking on buildings that were a good source of prey. I had to imagine they weren't carting the vagabonds they captured all that far before hauling them into Nidavellir. There'd even been a few of those symbols etched on a weathered post outside the main tunnel.

Not a hint of them inside, though. Just like the other eight locations I'd already poked about in. All in all, this expedition had been a flop.

Nothing else in the area seemed promising. With a huff, I pushed off the ground and strode up into the air, toward the glittering arc of the rainbow bridge Odin had left open for our use.

The dark elves were sneaky. We knew that. Still, it was difficult to ignore the urge to set a thing or two aflame to vent my frustrations. Not least because I had so many things to be frustrated about. I'd hoped the journey down here would wear away those bitter feelings, but they lingered on.

Blasted Hod. Blasted Baldur and Thor and Freya too. They had the truth of things right in front of them, had seen it with their own eyes, and still they didn't dare question their king. Wasn't questioning all they'd done with me since the moment I'd set foot in Asgard? Over and over again, as if they never quite trusted any of my answers no matter how many I gave them.

The realm of humans fell away under my soaring feet. I passed through the clouds in the space of a few heartbeats. The softer warmth of Asgard settled around me with a hint of wildflowers, but it didn't soothe my irritation.

The scent tugged at my memories. A yearning I

hadn't felt in decades, possibly centuries, rose up. Or perhaps it had been there all along, and I'd simply gotten so skilled at quashing it that I'd stopped noticing it.

As I crossed the last stretch of the bridge, I considered the city with its gleaming halls, so many of them vacant now. So many gods of Asgard who'd drifted away. Hadn't Thor and the rest ever thought to wonder why? *I'd* been glad enough to see most of them gone, but you'd think the others would have taken the time to wonder.

I veered to the left to skirt the edges of the city. Beyond a small span of forest lay an undulating field, the grass high enough to rustle against my calves as I stalked into it. Sprigs of clover and bluebells and dryas bloomed amid the thin strands.

On and on I walked, until the grass and the flowers thinned. Most of the vegetation gave way to bare earth mottled with stones, leading down to a desolate shore. Asgard's sea hissed over the pebbles.

The boulder stood there still, in the midst of that barren land. Claw marks too frantic and deep for time to have worn away decorated its lumpy surface. I rested my hand on the cool limestone and bowed my head.

I could still see the way my son had prowled around this boulder, hear the way he'd thrashed his wolfish body against the chains that bound him fast. Chains the dark elves had constructed for the gods with Odin's approval, if I recalled correctly. One more reason to want to bash the dirt-eaters' sallow skulls in.

He's a danger, the gods had all said. *A monster*. Fenrir

had been no more monstrous than I was. Which perhaps wasn't saying much. But we'd both been shaped into our villainy by the Allfather in his supposed wisdom, hadn't we?

If I'd stood up to him more firmly then, might I have spared my son his fate, even if I couldn't have changed my own path? I hadn't thought so back then, but it was hard not to wonder at times like this.

Prod and jab the ones you dislike until they lash out exactly as you intended, and then act out your horrified surprise: That was the Asgardian way.

My fingers curled as if I could stroke my son's thick fur across the ages. The way he'd looked at me when I'd first discovered him here back then, so furious and yet so pleading... My hand balled into a fist.

There was nothing to be done about it now. That was why I hadn't let myself dwell on things like this. But the raven's prison had stirred up far too many memories and brought them into sharply vivid being. I'd lived through too much of my past all over again to keep it buried.

The memories must have wrapped me up more tightly than I'd realized, because when a holler of my name carried across the field and I raised my head, the sky above me had dimmed to a purple bruise. I pushed away from the boulder and turned around.

Thor was marching across the field toward me. He slowed to an amble when he saw he had my attention. His ever-present hammer swung from his belt. I'd gone centuries without thinking about how I'd won him that damned thing, and now I couldn't look at it without feeling the fresh sting of a leather thread sewn across my lips.

"Here you are, Sly One," Thor said as he reached me. He surveyed the landscape with a mildly puzzled expression. "What on earth are you doing all the way out here?"

I glanced at the boulder. "I felt the need to remember. The urge has passed."

Thor followed my gaze, and a shadow crossed his face. "It was a nasty trick," he said. "I should have said so then."

"Too late for that now," I said, but without any rancor. A little of the tension wound up inside me eased. It said something that Thor could stand here and make a comment like that when the beast my son had become had been the one to ravage his own father. How eagerly had Odin welcomed those teeth, the ones he'd planned for and directed there himself?

Not to mention the fact that the Thunderer had died in battle with another of my children, each of them slaying the other. My offspring had gotten around during that fraught occasion. If Thor could let bygones be bygones, I couldn't hold much resentment toward him.

"What brings *you* out this way, old friend?" I asked, motioning him back toward the city.

"Freya noticed you returning from Midgard, but didn't see where you'd gone," Thor said as we headed toward home together. "I wondered if you'd discovered anything in your search down there."

"Alas, not today," I said. "There's altogether too much

Midgard. I have a few thoughts on where to search next, though."

Thor nodded. "If anyone can out-wile Surt and his allies, it'll be you."

We walked on in companionable silence, over the field and through the strip of forest. Thor turned down the pathway, I assumed making for his hall, and I stayed with him on my way to mine. We'd only gone a little farther when he raised his hand to the opposite twins of light and dark, who were standing in one of the smaller courtyards. Standing and looking as if they'd been waiting for us.

"Trickster," Hod said in a flat voice, and turned his blind gaze toward Thor. "Where had he slunk off to?"

"You could ask *me* that question," I said, but a prickling sensation shot over my skin. Why would he be asking at all, and asking that way?

He thought I'd been up to some mischief—or worse.

Had Thor come looking for me just to hear my news, or had the other gods sent him off to bring me back, to ensure I was staying in line? His company might not have been so companionable after all. My hackles rose.

"All right," Hod said. "What have you been doing all this time?"

"I spent most of the time on Midgard, as I said I was going to, if you'd been listening, Blind One," I said, managing to keep my voice even. "I investigated several promising locations and determined none of them hold a gate to the dark elves' realm. Not the most thrilling report, but crossing possibilities off our list is better than nothing."

"Freya saw you returning hours ago."

"Yes," I said, and maybe my tone turned a little snippy then. "I needed some time to my thoughts, like anyone does. Do you expect a full accounting of those too?"

"It was a simple question," Hod said, as if he were offended by my taking offense. "You can keep your thoughts to yourself, thank you."

"Strange," I couldn't help saying. "After all the hesitation you expressed earlier about carrying out interrogations, you seem to have no trouble when it comes to me."

Even Baldur's normally placid expression tensed. He raised his hand. "I don't think my brother meant—"

"You don't need to make excuses for him," I said. "His tongue is in perfectly good working order even if his eyes aren't. If he wants to explain himself further, let him do it."

"Loki," Thor said. Was that a *warning* in his voice? I gritted my teeth against the acrid retorts I could have made. One might have slipped free anyway if light footsteps hadn't pattered along the path toward us right then.

"What's going on?" Ari asked, her gaze darting between our faces as she came to a stop at the edge of our cluster. "Did something happen? Has Surt—"

Her panic dampened the anger that had been flaring inside me. I grasped her shoulder gently. "Nothing's wrong. There's no news from Midgard. All seemed well enough when I was down there. We were just having a little chat about unrelated topics."

Hod shifted his weight, but presumably he didn't want to look like an ass in front of our valkyrie. I didn't know how she'd managed to gain that kind of power over Mr. Dark and Prickly, but by some sort of magic over the last few weeks, she'd softened him. He inclined his head when her eyes moved to him again.

"It's about time for dinner, isn't it?" Thor the Ever Hungry rumbled, and that was an easy subject to agree on.

"Are you offering to host?" I asked. "Or should I ask, does your pantry hold enough to satisfy more appetites beyond your own vast one?"

He chuckled and waved us on down the path. "I'm sure I can scrounge up a few scraps to satisfy the lot of you."

"I've got fresh plums I could bring," Baldur offered, and diverted to his own home to retrieve them.

Ari glanced up at me as we meandered along, a hint of worry lingering in her eyes. "You're sure everything is fine? I'd like to be kept in the loop here."

"I promise, anything that relates to our impending war, you'll hear about it as soon as anyone," I said. "Eager to smash some more dark elf skulls, are we, pixie?"

She made a face at me, but at the same time she hooked her hand around my arm. "I'll be glad when we don't need to smash anymore. I'm just looking forward to getting to that point."

"All in good time," I said. "I told you they were right to be afraid of you."

She looked as if she were going to grimace again, but

her lips twitched into a smile so fierce it made my chest swell with affection to see it.

My valkyrie. And how well she'd done by us so far.

I only wished I could feel with confidence there was more than that one good thing in all of Asgard these days.

6

Aria

One thing I'd learned during my first venture into Valhalla, all by myself, was that I didn't need Odin's presence—or his permission—to go traveling down the branching path beyond the hearth. Without a hint of guilt, I slipped past the early morning sunlight drifting through the hall's windows and clambered through the opening at the back of the fireplace.

At the foot of Yggdrasil, the chillier air in the darkness there made me shiver. I focused on the rough but solid bark of the tree rather than the emptiness on either side of it, and set off. The branch Odin had pointed me to when I'd gone scouting in Muspelheim before was... this one.

I paused for just a moment at the base of the branch, willing my wings to emerge from my back. The straps of my racerback tank top twitched as the feathered edges brushed them. I touched my hair, making sure it was still tightly tucked into the ponytail I'd pulled it into. I didn't want there to be any chance of anything, including a stray hair, distracting me. My previous trip had made it clear that even a few seconds could make the difference between whether I returned or not.

Dragging in a breath that tingled through my lungs, I strode down the branch to the shadowy gateway at its end. Without giving myself a chance to consider any doubts, I plunged right through.

This time, I was ready for the rock dragon. The second I stumbled through into the hot sulfur-smelling air, I heaved myself back toward the cliff it had leapt at me from last time. A ragged protrusion offered a few ledges with a hint of shelter. I ducked under one and gripped the gritty rock, hugging the cliff-face as closely as I could.

There was a rasp and a warble of wind overhead as the dragon must have shifted from its perch. Its shadow swept over the barren plain below the cliff. But it didn't roar, and after a minute it wheeled around. The shadow disappeared as it settled back on the top of the cliff with a thump.

One hand and foot at a time, I eased myself down to the base of the cliff. Setting my shoes carefully to avoid any rattling of pebbles or stubbing of toes, I crept away, staying close enough to the cliff that the dragon shouldn't be able to see me unless it decided to do a second sweep.

By the time I reached a point where the cliff curved away from the area where I'd come out of the gate, sweat was trickling down my back. I hurried around the bend to where I'd be completely out of sight and then flapped my wings to send a cooling breeze over my skin, as much as it *could* cool me in this broiler of a realm.

There hadn't been any monstrous guards stationed between here and much closer to Surt's fortress last time, but I still kept my eyes peeled and ears perked as I lifted into the air and flew on toward the stone buildings I'd found the other day. I intended to get a better look at them this time—and to come back with some information we could actually use.

To show Odin that whatever information he was getting, staring down from his high seat, it wasn't enough.

I skirted the mountains I'd rambled through before and crossed the skeletal forest. The back of my neck itched more than once with the impression of being watched that was becoming annoyingly familiar. After whipping around a few times and not being able to spot any reason for worry, I resigned myself to just living with it.

If there was someone or something watching me, they hadn't bothered to attack me during my last trip or so far during this one. Maybe I was just picking up on the attention of some of the realm's more cautious inhabitants, ones who didn't want trouble any more than I did.

At the pointed hills I now knew Surt's fortress lay on the other side of, I took a diagonal route to my left. The uneven stone walls came into view just as I reached the low cliffs where the second dragon had come after me. Instead of venturing closer and risking drawing the attention of that beast or some other one, I glided onto a small protrusion and folded my wings against my back.

Loki had given me the sharpened senses the valkyries of the past would have used to scan battlefields and make their choices. I could put those to use here too.

I studied the shape of the fortress and every movement in and around it. As I intensified my gaze, more and more details came into focus across the distance. The guards by the walls were carrying weapons that reminded me of the ones the dark elves had come at us with the other day, the ones with the fiery burn. A sound reached my honed ears: a heavy clatter that made me think of a rockslide. It seemed to come from the direction of the fortress, but I couldn't make out its source.

I checked the top of the cliff for any sign of my draconic friend, and then I leapt to a ledge farther along, and then another, tipping my head to track the sound. It stopped for several minutes, so I stopped too. Then it came again, a little louder. Just over...

The acrid breeze tugged at my hair as I came to rest on a ledge even closer to the fortress. I braced my hands against the rough stone in case I needed to quickly spring away.

Just inside the fortress walls, at the edge of a lifeless courtyard, two figures emerged from a patch of darkness —a hole dug into the ground. They heaved a cart with them up a ramp set against the wall and dumped its contents over the top in a cascade of stones, some of them only pebbles, many as big as my head. A wide heap of rubble like that already rested against much of the outer side of that wall. They'd been excavating for a while.

Why? What else where they doing down in the tunnels they were digging? It had to be part of Surt's plan.

I was about to edge even closer when a dark shape dropped onto a spike of rock several feet away from me with a ruffle of black feathers. My body went rigid at the sight of the raven, my gaze twitching away from it and back. How had I not heard her sneaking up on me?

Muninn must be up to her old tricks again.

I tensed to lunge at her, and her form expanded, her feathers rippling away into strewn black hair and a loose black dress that made her pale limbs look gawkishly thin. The spear of stone she was perched on was barely wide enough for both of her human feet to fit on, but she managed to keep her balance there without any hint of a struggle. Her wide dark eyes were fixed on me.

"Hello, valkyrie," she said in her softly hoarse voice. "Has Odin sent you to play his raven now? His eyes and ears where he can't be?"

"Odin doesn't even know I'm here," I snapped. Maybe that hadn't been the smartest thing to admit, but I couldn't take the words back after they'd tumbled out. I adjusted my weight on the ledge. If I sprang fast enough, could I grab her and hope to hold her?

But even if I could, what would I do with her then? I could transport myself back to Valhalla in an instant, but I couldn't take her with me. Maybe if she'd been dead and I'd summoned her like a warrior of old... but I'd never tried *that* before, so probably this wasn't the best time to experiment.

Odin's former raven of memory wasn't our greatest enemy here. I wanted to know what she might reveal about Surt more than I wanted her dead for the way she'd tortured us. Although if she happened to die after I found out something useful, I wasn't going to cry about it.

"What do you want?" I said. "Did you figure you'd harass me a little more before you sound the alarm?"

"No," Muninn said. "I don't think Surt needs to know about this. I don't belong to him, you know. I had no need for a new master."

"You're doing him an awful lot of favors for someone who's not working for him."

She shrugged, her dress moving in a way that recalled ruffled feathers. "We work together, when it suits me. It suited me to see Odin brought down. It suited me to try to stop you from freeing him. That's done now. I've never had any particular grudge against you personally. You didn't choose to be a part of this either, did you?"

The cock of her head and the gleam in her eyes were oddly sympathetic. A prickling spread along the base of my wings. I wanted to fly away from her, and I wanted to fly *at* her and smack that hint of a smile off her face, but I wasn't sure I'd like the results of either act.

"You haven't answered my first question," I said. "What do you want?"

"You've looked around here," she said. "You've seen the devastation. Muspelheim wasn't pretty even when I first found myself here, you know, but things have gotten worse. The heat rises; the air grows drier; the magma flows faster. Barely anyone survives outside Surt's fortress."

"And they did before?" I said skeptically. I couldn't imagine this realm had ever been anyone's dream home.

"Some managed to make a bit of a life for themselves," Muninn said. Her gaze slipped away from me for a second, a shadow of melancholy passing over her face. Then her eyes jerked back to me. "No thanks to the gods."

"Do you really think letting this giant blaze his way across Asgard and Midgard is going to fix anything?"

"I don't know. It would at least be something different." She shifted closer to the cliffside on her precarious perch. "You're close with the gods who brought you to them. I saw that. But can you think beyond what they've told you? Can you consider that there may be other sides to the story?"

A sputter of a laugh escaped me. "Other sides? I don't think there's any way you can justify mass murder and the raising of those corpses into some kind of undead army."

"I'm not attempting to justify it," the raven woman said. "I simply mean to point out—have you heard the stories of the olden times? Did they tell you who crafted Thor's treasured hammer or Odin's great spear?"

I'd seen the end result of Loki's bargaining for those weapons in painful clarity in the memories she'd stirred up. "The dark elves," I said. "So what? That was ages ago, and it's not as if they did it out of the kindness of their hearts."

"They wanted to impress the gods. They often did.

You'll find many of the treasures of Asgard came from them, sometimes freely given. Relations between the gods and the dark elves used to be those of tentative allies, and the elves were always more eager for that alliance. You might ask yourself why they turned in a different direction now. No one enters a war for the fun of it."

"If you know why they're doing this, why don't you just tell me?"

Her lips curled in a faint grimace. "Would you believe it from me? I think not. Better you seek the dark elves out yourselves, hear the tales from their own lips. I only have scraps as it is."

Go to the dark elves and have a little chat about why they'd tried to kill me, threatened to kill my little brother, and *had* killed who knew how many people? Sure, that sounded like it'd be a lovely visit.

But the raven woman's comments niggled at me. I hadn't heard the gods discuss why the dark elves might have allied with Surt. I'd just assumed there'd always been animosity between Asgard and Nidavellir. If Muninn was right...

"Why are you telling me any of this?" I asked abruptly. "What does it matter to you what I think?"

Muninn gave another of her dress-ruffling shrugs and started to straighten up. "All I've ever really wanted was for something to change. It doesn't matter to me that much how. Perhaps all it'll take is one new spark in the mix."

Before I could push for more answers, she leapt off the cliff, contracting back into her raven form in the same moment. She flapped away with a hoarse caw. I moved to spring after her, and the rattle of claws against rock drew my gaze upward.

The dragon was lounging along the cliff-top just a short distance farther along. If I took after Muninn now, it'd spot me for sure.

My hands clenched into fists, but that niggling of uncertainty dug right down to my heart. Maybe this wasn't the place I'd get the rest of the answers I needed. What else could my gods tell me that they hadn't yet?

7

Aria

"There are a bunch of buildings," I said, adding some shapes to the rough layout of Surt's fortress I'd drawn. The rough pencil rasped against the faded strip of paper that Baldur had scrounged up. The gods might have had a perfectly modern house down in Midgard, but up here they were still kind of stuck in the old ways. Maybe I'd have to encourage a little updating of supplies. "I'd guess the biggest one in the middle is the one Surt rules from, but I didn't actually see him, as far as I know."

"And where were these excavations you witnessed happening?" Loki said as he leaned against the table in Valhalla where I'd spread the paper.

"Over here." I tapped the spot by my sketched wall and added a dark circle there. "I've got no idea what they're doing down there other than clearing out a larger space."

"He needs somewhere to keep that army," Thor rumbled with a frown. "Perhaps he creates more room as he adds to their number."

"Odin might have seen something," I said. "Or he could look from that high seat now and check things out. If he feels like telling us what he thinks is going on, that is." I still had my doubts about that. If he'd been able to watch the fortress at all, how could he have completely missed that activity? He'd probably just decided we didn't need to know about it.

Loki rubbed his narrow chin. "I do believe there's quite a network of existing underground tunnels throughout Muspelheim. Cooler and more protected than walking around in the open above ground."

"You speak from personal experience?" Hod asked, his tone dry. He was propped against the table opposite ours, since he couldn't see my drawing anyway.

"I have made a point of traveling nearly everywhere in the realms, both of my own accord and because the Allfather decided to drag me," the trickster said. "All the better for us."

"If we just attack his fortress, he could escape, then," I said. "Take off through the tunnels. We can't tear apart the whole realm, even with our combined power."

"Could we cut off the tunnels first, cause cave-ins or the like, before the main attack?" Baldur asked.

I blinked at him, startled to hear those words from him in that nonchalant tone. His tone was normal, but I couldn't remember hearing the god of light and harmony talking military strategy that blatantly before.

But then, he was also the god of justice. Sometimes justice required a sword.

"We'd need to know exactly where they all were," Loki said. "Leave one avenue open to him, and he'd slip through our fingers. He's proven himself awfully tricky for a giant. Not to mention the issue of the gates he's apparently built that fortress around. He could leap from there through any of them."

"He wouldn't be able to move an entire army through a gate at any speed," Hod said. "As long as we destroy his manpower, it doesn't matter that much how quickly we catch *him*."

"That's true," Thor said. "Cut off his might, and it's just a matter of tracking him down for the final blow."

Their comments stirred up my thoughts with the subject I hadn't yet mentioned. This was as good a time as any, wasn't it?

"Something else happened while I was in Muspelheim this morning," I said.

Hod's head snapped toward me in an instant.

Loki gave me an evaluating look. "Nothing too horrifying, I assume," he said lightly. "Seeing as you appear to have returned to us with all your parts intact. Why didn't you mention it earlier?"

I set down the pencil, fighting the urge to squirm in my discomfort. "I wasn't sure whether I should mention it at all. It was just— Muninn approached me. Just to talk."

Thor snorted. "That feathered fiend. She was looking to wrap you up in another tangle of memory, probably."

"That's what I thought at first," I said. "But the way

she was talking... I'm not sure what her motives were. But that doesn't mean she didn't say anything useful. She brought up the dark elves and how they used to be kind of allies of Asgard. Now they've turned against you—they're helping a guy who wants to destroy you. Why would they do that?"

"The dark elves have always been shaky allies at best," Thor said.

"That's pretty different from becoming an outright enemy."

"They've had plenty of time for resentments to fester," Loki said. "But I take it you believe it would help us to know which specific resentments are afflicting them?"

"I've just been thinking..." I made a face at the attempt at a map I'd drawn. "They're doing a lot of work for Surt. He's got other people guarding his fortress, but the dark elves are the only ones we've seen gathering humans for his draugr army, right?"

"They've always lived the closest to Midgard of all the realms' dwellers other than us," Baldur said.

"So it makes sense then," I said. "We wanted to close off all their access points, but maybe that's not really practical, or effective. They know we're looking for them now. They'll be sneakier. What if we could figure out why they've turned against you... and turn them back?"

"Then Surt loses his army supplies and all the other work they may have been doing for him, just like that." Loki snapped his fingers, a smile stretching across his face. "A truly cunning plan, pixie. I applaud you."

My skin warmed at his praise, but Hod looked

skeptical. "They've already gone this far," he said. "They've killed innocents and carted off their bodies to Surt. We've got no reason to think we've got anything we'd be willing to offer that would move them."

"It is difficult to appeal to someone's better nature if they don't appear to have one," Baldur put in.

"We should at least find that out, shouldn't we?" I said. "You don't know. I mean, come on, you all thought Loki had done horrible things for the sake of being evil, and it turned out he had other reasons. We obviously can't assume we know everything just from how it looks."

"A lesson you'd have thought this bunch would have learned by now," Loki said, a hint of acid in his tone.

The other three still hesitated. Thor ran a hand over his dark auburn hair. "That's a fair point. We don't know, so we should find out. It could be there's more to the situation than we realize."

Loki lifted his hands. "The voice of reason coming to us from the Thunderer! Who could have predicted that?"

Hod scowled at him, but he inclined his head in agreement. "All right. We'll be better off if we understand our enemies better. I won't argue against that."

"We might not even have to reach out to them at all," I said. "We can start by discussing it with Odin and seeing what he knows—"

"Discussing what?" a low voice carried from down the hall.

I jerked around. The Allfather had just stepped into Valhalla, the peak of his broad-brimmed hat nearly brushing the doorframe overhead. He made his way toward us with steady steps, the base of his spear tapping along against the wooden floor in time. It touched the ground so lightly he couldn't have been using it for any support. The sound felt more like a warning than anything else.

"Aria had a thought about the dark elves," Baldur started, but I set my hand over his to stop him. It was my idea; I should be the one to try to convince Odin.

"We should find out why they're helping Surt with his war," I said. "And then we can either win them back to our side or convince them they're better off if they stay out of it. Either one would leave him without his main helpers."

Odin raised the eyebrow over his good eye. "And what inspired this line of thinking?"

I braced myself against the bench. "I spoke to Muninn. In Muspelheim. I think... if we found the right angle, we might even be able to win *her* back to our side." Even though the thought of fighting alongside her again made my skin crawl, I couldn't deny that she must have all kinds of useful inside info about our main enemy.

Odin let out a dismissive chuckle. "She's made her allegiances more than clear. As for the dark elves, they've been jealous of our power since the beginning. Now they've finally been given a way to act on those feelings. There's nothing more complicated to it than that, and nothing we could offer them except our defeat."

"I think the valkyrie's point has some merit," Loki said quietly. "They did fashion that spear of yours. They've given us enough gifts over the ages."

"I've seen no reason to think the dark elves might be swayed," Odin said firmly.

Frustration prickled up my back. "You've seen a lot with all the traveling around I've heard you do, and with that high seat of yours," I said. "Even *I* can tell that things are getting worse in the other realms. You told us yourself that only this one and Midgard have stayed balanced—that's why Surt wants them. Why haven't we done anything about *that*? Why are the realms failing at all?"

"A lot of questions from one only so recently with us," Odin said dryly, but his single-eyed gaze felt heavy on me. "All things run down eventually. You should know that as well as anyone, being so recently mortal."

The reminder of my death made my shoulders stiffen, but I pushed myself off the bench so I could at least come closer to meeting him face to face. "That's a bullshit answer. 'All things run down.' Sure, but Asgard isn't. Midgard isn't. So what's different with the others?"

"If Nidavellir is failing as well, that could have pushed the dark elves to take more drastic action," Hod said, eyeing his father warily.

Odin made a sweeping gesture with his hand. "Our course is clear. Our enemies threaten us, and we must cut them off at the knees before they can. All this rambling only gives them more time to build their strength. Do you forget what they did to *me*?"

"Of course not," I said, struck by a sudden thought. "Why *did* they just keep you locked up? Why didn't they kill you while they had you? It seems like it would have made life a whole lot easier for them, if all they want is to destroy everyone here."

Odin's lips curled with what looked like disgust. "Surt was afraid that if he ended my life, I might be reborn in Asgard as before, outside his grasp, before he was ready to carry out the rest of his plans."

"Oh." I couldn't help asking, "Would you have been?"

"I don't know," the Allfather said darkly. "None of us knows our fate after this. Which is all the more reason we should follow the signs and recognize a day of reckoning is approaching, whether we like it or not."

"No," I said, taking a step toward him. Thor said my name like a plea and a warning combined, but I ignored him. They were too used to taking orders from Odin, but I didn't have that problem. "This is how you get your way with everything, isn't it? You act as if the future is set in stone, there's nothing anyone can do but accept the hand that's been dealt to us at face value and tackle it like that. Sounds like a really easy way to avoid responsibility for your choices to me."

"I only say what is," Odin said in a voice almost as thunderous as Thor's could be.

"Right," I said. "But you know what? If we'd thought like that when you were off in that cage of Surt's, you'd probably still be there, because we'd have given up and left you to the elves. So maybe that should be your hint that it's time to try a different way of looking at things. If you just—"

Odin cut me off with a smack of his spear against the floor. "I know what comes. We won't—"

A fierce cry and an ominous sounding thump carried through Valhalla's walls. My pulse hiccupped. All of us raced for the main doors in an instant, Loki speeding past the rest of us on his shoes of flight.

On the field that stretched between Valhalla and the forested fringe of the realm, Freya was flinging streaks of her magic, bright as her golden hair, at a group of lurching figures. As I pushed myself off the ground and flapped my wings to join the fight even faster, a putrid mildew-y stink filled my nose. The graying skin and bloated faces of her attackers confirmed my initial impression: They were draugr. Zombies who'd once been people like me.

My stomach lurched, but I whipped out my switchblade. They weren't human anymore. They weren't even really alive.

Loki gave a shout, and two of the undead forms burst into flames.

"We should come at them together!" Baldur called from somewhere at my other side.

A swatch of shadow had already toppled one of the others. Freya drew her sword and sliced the head off another. Jolted along by my surprise and fear, a bolt of lightning seared from my switchblade and blasted into the fifth. Thor's hammer smashed into the last of them a moment later.

I dropped to the ground near the scattered bodies, my chest heaving to catch my breath. Nothing else moved on the field beyond them.

Freya bent to tug something out of one of the fallen draugr's grasp. She held it up. It was a boxy metal device with an eerie red glow emanating from a sphere of glass at its center.

"I smelled them before I saw them," she said. "But it's a good thing I was nearby. This is dark elf work.

There was one of the dirt-eaters with the pack of them, but he ran off as soon as he saw me coming." She turned the device in her hand. "If I'm getting the right sense of this, one push of this button and the contraption would explode. They were heading for Valhalla."

A chill crept up my spine. The rest of us had been in Valhalla—had they known that and meant to kill us? Or had they simply been trying to cut off one of our main avenues into Surt's world?

"How did they reach this realm in the first place?" Loki said. "Let's see if we can't scrounge up that dark elf to tell us."

He darted forward, and the rest of us hurried after him. We didn't end up going far. Several feet from the edge of the forest, he stopped by a scorch mark that had blackened a strip of grass. A smoky smell rose off it. He prodded the burnt area with his toe.

Hod came up beside him and inclined his head. "What's the story of how Surt brought his army to Asgard during Ragnarok? Didn't he open a bridge of his own, one of fire?"

"He did," Thor said, his deep voice unusually subdued.

"Why did he only send seven people up here?" I said. "He couldn't really have thought he'd take us down with a little squad like that, could he?"

Odin's low voice carried from behind me. "It was a feint," he said. "He might have hoped they'd do some damage, but that wasn't the main purpose. The main purpose was testing how swiftly we'd react."

Loki grimaced. "And no doubt the dark elf that brought the draugr is reporting back to him right now."

"We fought them off," Baldur said, but with a hint of hesitation.

"You didn't use your combined power," Odin said. "The moment of a real fight, and you all reacted on your own."

"There was barely time," Hod started, and his father spun toward him with a singular glower.

"How much time do you expect Surt to give you? If we want to save this realm and Midgard, there's no more time for chatter. You should get back to your practice. We must be ready for our enemies." The Allfather cast one last look toward the scorch mark. "Foul giant."

I thought I saw Loki wince. But even I couldn't deny that we hadn't been completely ready for this tiny battle. I waved my switchblade with a crooked smile. "Time to bring out more targets?"

8

Thor

The sun had sunk almost to the distant treetops when I finished the last round of my patrol around the city. We couldn't know when Surt might make another attempt to breach our defenses. We had to be on guard now more than ever.

I found myself walking toward my father's hall rather than my own. All that time in Muninn's prison had brought up thoughts I hadn't considered in a long time. I'd tried to put them aside, but some of Odin's comments about Surt had stirred them up again. Maybe he could help set those thoughts to rest as well.

The hall was quiet, no one visible from the foyer. "Father?" I called out. He'd said he was going to survey the realms from his high seat—he might still be up there.

I swung my hammer as I waited to see if he'd come, taking reassurance from the heft of Mjolnir in my hand.

It *was* strange to think I relied so much on this weapon the dark elves had crafted, when they'd been the ones most frequently toppled by it in the last few weeks. And now they were leaving bombs on our doorstep.

Maybe Ari was right—maybe we should dig deeper into why. It certainly couldn't hurt to know more.

That principle was why I was here right now.

My stomach grumbled, reminding me that it had been several hours since lunch and at least two since my ample mid-afternoon snack. I'd almost made up my mind to leave and stop by again after I'd refilled my stomach when a faint creaking drifted from deeper within the hall. Odin must be descending the ladder that led to his upper floor.

He appeared in the hallway a moment later, his weathered face weary but his posture still straight. His spear gleamed in his hand, not quite touching the floor as he strode toward me.

"You wanted to speak to me, my son?" he said, his tone unreadable.

"If I'm interrupting you..." I started.

He waved his hand dismissively before I could continue. "A small break will do me good. A bit of rest for this overworked eye." The arch of his eyebrow seemed to say that he didn't really think he needed rest at all. He motioned me toward one of the side rooms. "Did you uncover something in your rounds?"

"No," I said. "All looks normal, except for that burn where Surt's bridge must have touched our land."

Odin nodded. "I hadn't realized he might summon that type of fire on his own. With the chaos during

Ragnarok, I never determined exactly how it had been formed—I assumed there was other effort involved."

My gut clenched at that idea. "Maybe there was again."

"I think not." The Allfather sat himself down on one of his fine wooden chairs and motioned me to another nearby. "I may not be able to watch everything at all times, but I haven't seen him associating with any allies of that stature. Only the dark elves and the riffraff he's gathered from Muspelheim. What matter did you wish to bring to my attention, then?"

"I only wondered..." I shifted on the chair, not sure how to proceed. "It may seem out of the blue, but I think it's time. We've never really talked about my mother."

Odin paused in the middle of adjusting his grip on the spear. He peered at me with his single brown eye for a long moment. "Did Muninn show you something distressing in that prison of hers?"

"No," I said. "I simply—I know she was a giantess. I have some kind of connection to Jotunheim. I thought, if I understood that better, perhaps it could help in defeating Surt." And in simply feeling more at peace with who *I* was, although I wasn't sure my father would see that as worthy reasoning. If Thor the Thunderer didn't know who he was by now, what could help me?

Odin let out a huff of breath. "There's nothing to be gained in speaking of her. It was a moment of ill-judgment on my part—although I have always been pleased with the result." He tipped his head to me. "I removed you from the giants' grasp the moment you were born. You are all mine and not at all theirs, down to your nature. I've had all the time in the world to observe it."

Those words didn't comfort me the way they might have once. I pushed onward. "There are still things I'd like to know. How did you come to, ah, meet her? What family was she of? Did—"

"Enough." Odin held up his hand, a definitive end to the conversation. He heaved himself back onto his feet. "You left that part of your life behind almost from the instant your life began. Leave it where it belongs. These are a people who can barely see two feet beyond their lusts and rages, other than those rare exceptions like Loki. We won't glean anything from them when they can barely glean anything of themselves. I should return to my searching."

He headed off toward the room that led to his high seat at a pace that offered no room for compromise. This was obviously a subject he had no intention of speaking on.

I frowned as I let him go. That remark about Loki brought back all the things the trickster had shown us in Muninn's construct of the room at the top of Odin's hall. The things my father had held his silence about for so very long. How many other secrets was he keeping?

But now didn't feel like the time for attempting to pry them loose. Not when Surt was sending his rotting army right to our back door. And I couldn't say Odin was wrong about the giants. By Hel, we'd been able to fool them into taking me for Freya with nothing but an ill-fitting dress and a veil that barely hid the battle fury in my eyes. By all evidence, most giants only saw what they wanted to see.

That fact settled deeper into my mind as I left the Allfather's hall. We'd deceived the giants so many times in the past. I wasn't sure we could trick Surt very easily— for him to have captured my father at all, he was clearly one of the sharper ones. But his kin back in Jotunheim... How might they play into this war?

Freya was just coming out of her hall a little farther into the city. She glanced at me and then past me to where I'd come from, and ambled over to join me.

"Did you talk to him?" she asked.

"Briefly," I said. "He was in a hurry to get back to his seat."

She hummed and sucked in her lower lip. "How did he seem to you?"

How could I answer that? The Allfather might have been my literal father, but his moods had always been nearly impenetrable to me. He kept his own counsel— that much had always been true.

"Concerned, but not overly so," I said, taking my best stab at answering. "A little tired. Impatient, but then, that's hardly unusual."

"He has all the patience in the world for his questing," she muttered, but there wasn't much rancor in her voice. "He's been quieter than usual even with me since we returned. I don't know how concerned *I* should be."

I didn't remember the goddess ever confiding that much to me before. Which suggested she was at least twice as worried as she was admitting.

"He's been through a lot," I said. "And there's a lot we still have to face. It'd be strange if he seemed completely normal."

"I know."

I hesitated and then offered the only comment I could think of that might make her feel better. "I'm concerned about him too. We're all keeping an eye on him."

"Some of us with different motives," she said with a hint of tartness. I wondered who she was talking about, but her expression had softened at the same time. "I suppose we'll see our way through this as we have so much else."

Before I could think of anything reasonably articulate to say in response, the smell of roasting meat wafted past my nose. An answering gurgle sounded in my belly. I was turning toward the scent before I'd even realized I was moving.

Freya laughed. "Let's see what we can ferret out for dinner, shall we?"

The savory smoky smell led us to Baldur's gleaming white hall. Around the back of it, we found him and Hod and Ari standing around a fire pit. A pig's carcass hung on a spit over the flames, its flesh browned and sizzling.

"It appears you have more than you can chew here," I said as I joined them.

Hod turned his head toward my voice. "Why am I not surprised that you showed up the moment the meal was ready?" he said with a smile.

"You know me too well."

"Just be sure you leave some for the rest of us."

"Ah, I don't believe I've ever downed more than half a roast pig in one meal."

I aimed a wink Ari's way. She grinned, but her expression looked a bit tight.

She'd taken on so much since we'd returned—and really before that too. All her solitary patrols of Muspelheim, having to contend with that raven woman and the other threats there on her own... I bristled instinctively, thinking about it.

Baldur moved to adjust the spit and check the meat, and I came to stand beside Ari, resting my hand on her shoulder with a gentle squeeze. She set her hand over mine. The simple sensation of her thumb tracing over the back of my hand sent a bolt of desire through me.

I kept those impulses in check, just enjoying the warmth of her touch. There'd be time to enjoy more with her, if she wanted, after other appetites were sated.

Hod had joined Baldur by the fire. He nudged his twin companionably as they discussed the state of the roast: Baldur going by sight and Hod by smell. Baldur's face lit up with a laugh.

When was the last time I'd seen them look so easy with each other? Definitely not since the mistletoe catastrophe. There'd always been a thread of tension between them from the moment of our rebirth. And if I'd picked up on it, then it hadn't been exactly subtle.

Now, despite this morning's attack, they appeared relaxed. Comfortable with each other.

My heart swelled with fondness. My brothers deserved that happiness after the struggles they'd been through.

Ari leaned over to kiss my knuckles. I couldn't resist drawing her chin up to kiss her properly. Her soft lips parted against mine, and right then I couldn't imagine how this place had felt complete without her.

She beamed at me, looking more relaxed herself at least for the moment, and went to grab the plates from the stone table nearby. "Isn't it about time we get carving that up? I'm starving."

"Let me," I said, moving forward. Baldur stepped aside with an amused expression and handed me the knife.

"Maybe you should take your portion last," he said teasingly. I couldn't remember the last time he'd poked fun either. Yes, we'd come through Muninn's tortures stronger.

"That's just asking him to eat everything that's left," Hod said with a laugh.

"We do need to keep our Thunderer well-fueled," Freya said, patting my arm.

I mock-glowered at them and dug the blade through the crackling skin. Juice seeped out to hiss in the fire, the sharper scent making my mouth water.

The pig tasted even better than it smelled, I discovered a few minutes later when I got to dig into the haunch I'd claimed. The flesh was just the right mix of chewy and tender, with a smoky flavor laced through the near-sweetness of the pork. I was about to go for a second helping when a tall slender figure with hair as bright as the flames in the fire pit emerged from the dusk.

"Well," Loki said, with a smile that looked as if it'd been cut into his face by a blunt knife. He came to a stop at the edge of our circle. "What a fine dinner I wasn't invited to."

Hod set down the plate he'd been holding. "Oh, don't sulk," he said mildly. "We are allowed to occasionally keep things in the family."

Loki's smile turned even stiffer. "The family," he repeated.

Ari swatted Hod's arm and motioned Loki over. "I don't think any formal invitations went out. Everyone just showed up."

"There's plenty more," I said, moving to the roast like I'd planned to anyway. The last thing we needed was the trickster in a mood. "I'll carve you a slice."

A minute later, Loki had a plate with a fine cut of pork on it. He considered it with a vaguely dissatisfied expression. I had no idea what the Sly One wanted now, so I just worked on chopping myself off the other haunch.

"After this morning's brief adventure, I think we need to talk strategy," Loki said. He started to pace around the fire pit. "Surt is getting bold. He must be close to ready to launch his full attack. Just barreling in there with our unified powers isn't likely to win the day."

"I assume you've come with your own ideas on that front," Freya said.

Loki gave her only the briefest nod of acknowledgment before barreling on with even more frenetic energy than he usually showed. "We need to step up our efforts to close off the gates to Midgard. Regardless of the dark elves' motives, which it may do us well to uncover, humankind is too vulnerable for them to have free access. Muninn may also be key, if we can contrive a way to capture *her*."

The beginnings of the idea that had been forming in my head earlier rose up. I lowered the carving knife. "There's also—When it comes to giants—"

Loki brushed me off with a flick of his hand. "Yes, yes, we know Surt is a giant. I have plenty of experience to draw on. We're well covered in that department."

"No," I said, a little more firmly. "I don't mean that. I was thinking about the time we faced Thrym and—"

"Come on now, Thunderer," Loki said. "This really isn't the time for reminiscing about past glories. If Surt was simply looking to marry Freya, we'd have a much easier situation on our hands. Now, when it comes to Muninn, she's clearly shown she's willing to talk to Ari..."

Hod jumped in to say that by no means should we be using our valkyrie as bait, and Ari argued that she could hold her own, and Freya wanted to return to the problem of sealing the gates on Midgard. No one looked to me, standing there with my half-carved haunch. An itch of frustration ran over my skin.

Why should they look to me? I wasn't known for my scheming or my strategic prowess. They needed me to hurl my hammer on the battlefield in whatever direction they pointed me.

But there was an ache in my gut, a different sort of hunger than I'd ever felt before. What if I wanted to be more than that? Where in the realms did I even start?

9

Aria

I should have been able to sleep. I had the whole damned hall to myself—one that had previously belonged to some lesser goddess whose fate I hadn't really wanted to ask about—including the softest bed I'd ever had the pleasure of sleeping on. The night outside the window was still and quiet. Any chill it had brought, the blanket I was snuggled under protected me from.

But still, I'd been lying there for at least an hour with nothing to show for it but the groove I was probably wearing into the mattress with all my tossing and turning.

When we'd first gotten back to the real Asgard, there'd been a moment or two when I'd thought maybe I didn't need an actual building as a home of my own. What would be the point when I could just hop from one of my gods' beds to another depending on the night? But

then as that first full night had gotten closer, I'd felt
edgier and edgier about the idea of settling down to sleep
the whole night next to anyone at all. Across all the one-
night stands I'd had since I'd moved out of my mother's
house, I'd never stuck around to cuddle.

What I had with the four gods who'd summoned me
was different from that. I couldn't deny it. But it was also
new and a little unsettling. To be practically *living*
together... No. I didn't even know what to call this yet. I
needed a place where I didn't have to think about it.

Which had worked out fine the first few nights, but
now apparently I had too many other thoughts chasing
each other around my mind.

I burrowed my head in the plump pillow and
squeezed my eyes tighter shut, as if that would bring
sleep on faster. After another couple minutes, I groaned
and shoved myself into a sitting position. My jaw creaked
with the size of my yawn. But still my head was buzzing
with the memories of my latest trip to Muspelheim, the
things Muninn had said, the attack by the draugr.

What if Surt sent a force like that into Midgard? We
couldn't keep watch over that entire realm as well as
Asgard. Muninn knew about Petey. She'd shown me his
foster home in her prison, lifted from my and the gods'
memories of the place. What if she pointed him there?

I rubbed my bleary eyes. Why would she do that?
She had to know it'd only make me ten times more
furious. If she'd wanted to threaten me, to hold his safety
over my head, she could have done it this morning. I had
to be here, and rested enough to fight properly, if I was
actually going to protect my brother.

Maybe, as exhausted as I felt, it wasn't exhausted enough. I pulled on some clothes and walked down the hall, figuring I'd swoop around over the city for however long it took before I was barely keeping my wings unfurled. I slipped past the door—and froze on the first tile of the path outside.

Odin was stalking down Asgard's main throughway, his cloak swaying in his wake, his hat pulled low even though there was no sun to guard against. He was already most of the way to the rainbow bridge, well past my hall. Where the hell was he going at this time in the night that he couldn't just spy on from his high seat?

I hesitated for only a second longer, and then I darted after him, setting my feet softly on the stone tiles.

I stayed far behind Odin as I followed him, sticking to the deeper shadows around the buildings. When he strode onto the faint glimmer of his rainbow bridge, I waited until he'd just disappeared over the crest of it and leapt into the air with a light flap of my wings. By the time I'd glided over the bridge, he'd descended almost to the ground. He unfurled the last length of the bridge, which he'd contracted earlier so no dark elves could clamber up to Asgard that way, and set off across the tilled farmland where he'd set it down.

The rolling fields made it easy to keep an eye on his tall form even in the night. Wherever we'd ended up, it was warmer than it'd been in Asgard, the air sharp with heat despite the darkness. A half-moon shone starkly overhead. Only a faint breeze rustled the stalks of the plants below me. I flapped my wings cautiously, trying to make as little sound as possible. My valkyrie powers might make me invisible to any mortal unless I wanted to be seen, but I doubted that worked on the Allfather.

He paused once, and then again several minutes later, cocking his head as if listening for something. I couldn't hear anything other than the occasional rumble of a truck passing along the two-lane highway nearby. Both times he veered a little more to the right.

We passed a few houses that gave me the impression we were in some other country. I'd never seen any in that style back home. After a while, we crossed the highway and rambled over a couple of low hills. The vegetation turned scruffier, dry earth dotted with weeds and prickly shrubs.

At the top of the third hill, a dusty shack stood next to a shriveled tree. Odin slowed. I eased down to the ground and crouched behind one of those thorny bushes to watch.

He paced around the shack and a little farther down the other side of the hill. Whatever he found there made him come to a halt. His head bowed in apparent contemplation. He rubbed his bearded chin. I thought I could make out a frown on his worn face.

My legs were starting to get stiff in their cramped position by the time he returned to the shack. He circled it once more, slowly, his single eye narrowed. He appeared to examine the tree in turn. Then, with a sigh I could hear even from my hiding place, he headed back the way he'd come.

I tensed behind the shield of my shrub, but Odin stalked down the hill a few dozen feet from where I was crouched without glancing my way. When he'd reached the bottom of the hill, I eased around the bush and crept up to the shack myself. What the hell had he been looking at?

It didn't take long to figure it out. Over the other side of the hill, the cracked earth was blackened with a scorch mark like we'd seen in the field in Asgard—the one Surt's bridge of fire had left behind. Had this been its starting point?

An uneasy shiver crawled over my skin. I rubbed my arms as I took to the air again. If Surt and his undead soldiers were lurking around here, I didn't want to be caught on my own.

How had Odin known about this place? Why had he come down just to look at it?

Somehow I had the feeling he wasn't going to answer those questions willingly. I'd bet he didn't plan to even mention this little trip to the rest of us tomorrow.

I had to fly a little faster than before to catch up with Odin. I wasn't sure enough of the path we'd taken to find my way back to the bridge on my own. He strode over the hills and across the farmers' fields at a swifter pace than before, now that I guessed he'd found what he'd been looking for. This time, he didn't stop to consider his direction at all.

When the sheen of the rainbow bridge came into sight up ahead, I eased up completely, dropping down onto the thick lower branch of a waxy-leafed tree. I might as well let him go on ahead of me before I followed, now that I knew my way home.

It was a good thing that I did. I'd just settled onto the branch when Odin jerked around. He peered back across the field. I went rigid, holding my muscles still and my breath in my chest, shadowed by the leaves around me. His gaze seemed to pass over the tree, but it didn't stop there. Finally, he started walking again.

What was he afraid of?

He reached the rainbow bridge and started up it, the base of it fading in his wake. Just a hint of it remained below the streak of clouds he disappeared into.

As soon as he was out of sight, I sprang into flight. The swoop of my wings brought me up to the bridge. I peeked cautiously through the haze of the clouds to see the Allfather's peaked hat just vanishing over the crest of the bridge.

I soared the rest of the way to Asgard, the cooler wind there buffeting my wings. Odin was out of sight by the time I reached the city. Back to his hall to get some sleep —or to spend more time spying on the world from that magical seat of his?

I'd hoped going out to fly would burn off some of my uneasy energy. Instead I'd ended up feeling even more wired than before. My pulse rattled through my veins as I headed down the street. I had too many questions jostling around with the worries in my head, and my mind was getting too foggy to sort them out.

My heart tugged me toward one of the other buildings along the main road. I hesitated outside the door to Thor's hall, but the longing inside me propelled me onward.

I didn't know where my place was here, now that

Odin was back and calling so many of the shots. I had no idea what the future might hold for me or any of the gods I'd started to think of as mine. But the thunder god wasn't part of any of those conflicts. Thor came with no dark secrets, no furtive motives. He liked me, he wanted me, nothing more complicated about it than that.

It was easy to find his bedroom. The low rumble of his sleeping breath carried through the doorway. I slipped inside to find him sprawled on his back across a gigantic bed made to fit him. His brawny form almost filled the whole thing anyway, but that was fine. I didn't need much room.

I eased under the blanket and tucked myself in next to him, leaning my head against his shoulder. I hadn't meant to wake him up, but Thor shifted onto his side at my touch, his arm sliding around my waist.

"Ari?" he murmured sleepily.

I nestled closer to his muscled chest. A momentary panic clenched around my lungs—what was I doing here? Why had I given in to this impulse? What was he going to think it meant? But at the same time, the warmth of his body soothed my nerves.

This was Thor. He'd think it meant what I told him it meant.

And I needed this right now.

"I couldn't sleep," I said. "I just... I wanted to be somewhere I feel safe."

A pleased hum emanated from the thunder god's throat. He bent his head to kiss my forehead. "You'll always be safe here," he said.

I wasn't sure that was true, as much as he might have

wanted it to be. At that moment, it felt as if it could be right, and that was enough. His hand stroked over my hair, and my eyelids drooped, and for the first time all night my body relaxed. In the temporary peace of Thor's arms, I drifted off to sleep.

10

Aria

I might have been nervous about falling asleep next to any of the gods, but there was something very appealing about waking up next to one of them.

I eased into awareness with Thor's tangy scent in my nose and those solid muscles pressed up against me. In my sleep, one of my legs had ended up tucked between his. Heat pooled between my thighs when I adjusted my position, and Thor let out a ragged breath. The evidence of his own arousal rested against my hip.

"Good morning," he said, his voice so thick with desire it sent an eager shiver down to my core.

"Very good," I said, and scooted up his body to capture his mouth with mine.

Thor kissed me back hungrily, but his hand stayed gentle as it skimmed down my back. It came to a stop at the waist of the jeans I hadn't bothered taking off when

I'd crawled into bed with him. His thumb teased over the skin of my back with an electric tingle where my shirt had ridden up.

I traced my fingers up to his sculpted shoulders. My nipples hardened where they brushed against his chest through my shirt. I was just about to strip that shirt off so I could enjoy him skin to skin when a singsong voice called from outside.

"Oh, pixie! Ready for today's mission?"

From Loki's wry tone, I suspected he could guess that I wasn't particularly ready. But we *had* agreed last night that I'd help him track down another of the dark elves' gates today, and the sooner we got started on that, the safer Midgard would be. Protecting Petey was a heck of a lot more important than scratching this itch—as much as my body protested as I pulled away from Thor.

"Coming!" I hollered back.

The thunder god groaned as he sat up beside me. "Wretched giant," he muttered good-humoredly, but the words reminded me of Odin's remark about Surt yesterday. I hoped Loki's hearing wasn't quite good enough to have caught this one.

"You've survived how many eons without me around?" I said. "You can probably make it through a few hours more."

"That doesn't mean I *want* to," Thor said with a grin.

He looked so pleased with himself for that remark that I had to lean in for one more kiss. The sweep of his tongue over mine was a promise of more to come whenever we picked up where we'd left off.

Loki was standing on the tiled road outside the front

door, his lips curled with amusement. "I apologize if I interrupted anything," he said, sounding not at all sorry.

"How did you even know where—" I started, and then remembered. I'd tried to take off on the gods once, after the dark elves had threatened Petey, and the trickster god had tracked me down without any trouble at all. He was the one who'd chosen me, who'd focused their powers when they'd summoned me and recreated me as a valkyrie, so the tie between the two of us ran even deeper than with the others.

Which wasn't really a bad thing. I couldn't think of anyone other than him more likely to get me out of a sticky situation, if I happened to find myself in another one I couldn't get out of on my own.

"I don't monitor you that closely," he said, motioning me along with me. "But you weren't at your own hall when I came calling there first."

"I had trouble sleeping," I said, as if he needed an explanation.

"And I'm sure joining the Thunderer in his bed was wonderfully restful."

I elbowed him in the arm, a little harder than I would have if he hadn't been an essentially immortal being. "It was, actually. A lot more than if I'd tried to snuggle up with *you*, I'm sure."

"Oh, I would have made sure you didn't regret that choice." His smile stretched wider as we headed down the road toward the bridge. He handed me a bundle of fabric. "I assume you haven't had breakfast yet."

The napkin fell open to reveal a roll filled with cheese. I dug into it, finishing it by the time we'd reached the glimmer of the rainbow. The pinch of hunger in my stomach subsided, but a different tightness gripped my gut. None of the other gods knew where Odin had gone last night, I didn't think. I wasn't sure what there was to tell yet, though. He hadn't done anything *wrong*.

"How are we going to do this?" I asked instead. The last time we'd gone searching for dark elves, I'd piggybacked Loki so he could speed us along while I used my valkyrie senses to search for the dark elves' distinctive oily energy. It wasn't the most dignified position, though.

"I suppose I could carry you over-the-threshold style," the trickster suggested with an arch of his eyebrows.

I wasn't sure that would be all that more dignified, and it'd definitely be more of a distraction. "Maybe we should stick with piggyback."

He chuckled. "Whatever suits you, pixie."

With his elbows hooked under my knees and my arms looped loosely around his shoulders, he leapt into the air. I'd forgotten how quickly he could move when he wasn't holding himself back for the rest of us. The wind warbled past us, tossing my hair. In just a few seconds, we'd crossed the rainbow bridge and were speeding through the sky above the Midgardian landscape that sprawled toward the haze of the horizon.

I let my awareness stretch out toward the streets and buildings we soared past. Flickers of energy touched my senses, most of it the soft brightness I felt from human beings. I caught one flash of something thicker, but only a single form. We were looking for somewhere that several dark elves had congregated around.

"I'm covering new territory, separate from the areas

we perused last time," Loki said. "No point in retreading over old ground." It was the first time he'd spoken since we'd left Asgard. The muscles in his back shifted against my chest as he veered to avoid a looming mountain. Was he being quiet because of the exertion, or was something bothering him?

The sight of the land rushing away beneath us reminded me of last night's flight again. I rested my chin by the crook of Loki's neck, letting the spicy smell of him, like fire-warmed ginger and cardamom, wash over me. If anyone in Asgard knew better than to unquestioningly trust Odin's decisions, it was the god holding me.

"Do you really think that blocking the dark elves' gates is going to fix very much?" I asked.

He shrugged, shifting me closer to him as he did. "They're harming people. When it comes to that, you have to set down restraints, regardless of what their motives might be. I can't blame the gods for how they handled me after I completely committed to my role."

I didn't think I wanted to know what complete commitment had involved. I hugged his shoulders a little tighter. "What did they do?"

"Oh, I was chained up to a rock in a rather dank cave with a snake dripping poison on my face. Not memories I like to dwell on."

I shuddered at even the vague picture his words drew up. The slight edge in his voice made me suddenly sure he'd *had* to dwell on those memories not that long ago.

"Muninn sent you back to that time, didn't she?"

"Briefly," he said. "I endured it then for Norns only know how long—a small second helping wasn't too heavy a burden." He gave my calf a light squeeze. "You don't need to worry about me, pixie. They did what they had to do. Just as we're doing what we have to do. What's driving the dark elves, we can sort out once they're no longer terrorizing the populace."

I did worry about him, whether he liked it or not. Especially when I knew how good the trickster was at hiding how deeply things affected him. I opened my mouth to say something along that line—and a trickle of viscous energy licked over me. I stiffened, and Loki glided to a half.

"Do you feel something?" he asked.

I focused all my attention on the direction that sensation had arrived from. We were poised over ruddy desert now. The impression of several pulses of dark elf life reached me from the base of a mesa to our left. As I traced them, a couple disappeared, and two new impressions emerged in their place. I swallowed hard.

"I think we've found our gate."

———

With Odin's blessing, the six of us were able to emerge from Asgard over the desert plain almost instantly from the rainbow bridge. We hovered above the dry earth and plateaus of reddish rock for a moment to get our bearings.

"So we just rush right in and blast them like before?" I asked. I agreed with everything Loki had said before, but at the same time the idea didn't sit completely right with me. The dark elves weren't going to be too keen on having any kind of conversation with us if we kept slaughtering them on sight.

Maybe they deserved it. On the other hand, that was probably how the gods had felt about Loki, and taking a heavy hand with him had led straight up to the end of the world, as far as I could tell.

"If they don't attack us, there won't be any need to blast anyone except the guards," Hod said beside me, but he turned his gaze my way. "Unless you've sensed something that suggests we should be more cautious in our approach?"

I couldn't offer anything except for my general sense that Odin knew a shitload more about this situation than he'd been sharing with us, but that wasn't concrete enough to hang a hat on. I wet my lips, willing the nervous patter of my pulse to even out. "No. Not so far."

"Let's move in then," Freya said, brandishing her sword with a gleam of her magic.

"When I give the battle cry, the five of us attack together," Thor reminded us. "We took them down last time without even knowing how to use our combined power. This time should be even easier."

I nodded. Baldur shot me a smile like a beam of light. "We've got this."

We swooped down toward the spot I'd indicated, the base of a ruddy mesa with a sprinkling of green on its high flat top. As we sped toward it, a dabbling of shadowed cave entrances came into view, along the ground and up to several feet higher. In the middle of them lay a craggy opening with that ominously deep blackness I'd felt from the gate on the other hillside.

If that wasn't enough to identify our target, several dark elves stood in the shadows of the rocky outcroppings around it. The daggers and spears clenched in their pale hands shimmered with the same fiery energy as those some of the elves who'd come at us last time had carried. Weapons charged with Surt's searing magic.

Thor bellowed, and I slashed my switchblade through the air. This time, none of that lightning I still didn't know how to consciously summon leapt from my fingers. But it didn't matter. I was flinging myself into the fight, and four heartbeats around me thumped in time with my intentions.

A swath of shadow-tangled fire crackled over the guards. Thor's hammer whirled into their midst trailing knives of light. The flames whipped faster as the hammer passed through them, and a dark blaze formed around Mjolnir itself. When the flaring of light and dark faded, the guards' bodies were scattered, smoking, across the dusty ground around the gate.

That small contingent hadn't stood a chance against all of us in sync.

We landed in a semi-circle, braced for a fresh wave of attack. I scanned the caves with my valkyrie sensitivity. "There are a few more here," I said. "It doesn't feel as if they're moving. I don't know what they're doing."

"Maybe lurking with more of those explosive contraptions," Thor muttered.

"All right then, dirt-eaters!" Loki called out in a tone that was somehow dark but jovial at the same time. "Show yourselves, and we won't be forced to burn you right out of your hidey-holes."

A shuffling sound reached my ears. We all turned toward it, and the shadow at Baldur's feet rippled. A clump of grass it touched shriveled. What the hell? My gaze jumped up and caught on the clenching of his hand. Was he okay?

I didn't have the chance to find out right then. Four rounded faces topped with black hair appeared at the entrance to one of the caves farther down the side of the mesa. All four of the dark elves had their hands raised in a gesture of appeasement.

"Please," the young man at the front said, his expression tight. "Just let us get back to Nidavellir before you close it up. That's all we want."

The woman just behind him snatched at his sleeve. "What? No. What's the point? We're better off staying here."

His eyes widened as he looked back at her. "But—it's home," he said quietly.

Her mouth opened and closed again. "Is anywhere really home now?"

She sounded so hopeless it wrenched at me. Freya clapped her hands. "Make up your minds what you want, or you won't be around long enough to get anything at all."

The man tugged at the woman's hand, and her head bowed. They and their two companions dashed through the gate's opening.

"They'll bring more guards!" Thor protested.

I readied my blade, but no one emerged from the darkness of the elves' realm. An uncomfortable ache crept through my chest.

Some of the dark elves were vicious. Some of them had delighted in hurting us. The woman who'd taunted me about Petey came to mind. But that bunch—they'd seemed so torn, so worn down...

My gaze slid toward Hod, who was still at my right. His mouth had curved into a frown.

"We sealed one before with our powers combined," Loki said, striding forward. "Let's see if we can conjure up the same effect again."

I shook off as much of the creeping dread as I could. "On Thor's cue?"

Thor raised his hammer, and his cry echoed through me and the others, shaking off most but not all of the heaviness that had settled around my heart.

11

Hod

My footsteps thudded dully across Valhalla's worn floorboards, as if they knew I wasn't meant to be there. I might be able to fend for myself as needed, even contribute to a larger battle, but no one would ever mistake me for a warrior. The lingering scent of now-stale mead made my nose itch. But this was the fastest way to get where I wanted to go.

There'd been plenty of drinking a couple hours ago. By the time we'd returned to Asgard, the spirit of victory had taken hold. We'd feasted and laughed, and if Ari had seemed a little more reticent than usual, I could have blamed it on the stress of the last few weeks.

I didn't actually believe that was all it had been, though. Since I'd turned in for the night, or at least attempted to, I'd had two voices cycling through my head. Our valkyrie's, saying, *We obviously can't assume we know everything just from how it looks.* And that of the dark elf woman hesitating by the gate: *Is anywhere really home now?*

Something wasn't right. Something more complex than the jealousy my father had blamed for the dark elves' betrayal. The sense of it gnawed at my bones.

I should have been able to go to Odin with that understanding. Should have been able to trust that his wisdom would guide us. But look where trusting him had gotten us so far. When was the last time he'd given us a straight answer? He'd been there to meet us when we'd stepped off the bridge with claps on our shoulders and that warm Allfatherly praise he could pull out when the situation called for it. Proud and benevolent.

What a crock. The bastard had ordered my death over a murder *he'd* all but orchestrated. To restore the fucking balance, to set the stage he wanted for Ragnarok —who in the realms knew? I doubted he'd ever own up to the truth.

I stopped at the smoky smell that clung to the hearth area and forced myself to exhale slowly. Forced my fingers to retract from where they'd started to dig into my palms.

That kind of anger wasn't going to serve me well. When this war was over, my father and I would hash out all of this, calmly but definitively. Odin wasn't going to listen to raging or ranting. I had to draw on the cool stillness of the shadows I carried with me.

Especially now. I traced my hand along the polished stones of the hearth and ducked beneath them. Cinders crunched under my boots. Silence closed in around me as my feet hit the rough bark of Yggdrasil's path.

What I was about to do might be foolhardy, but on the other hand it might very well be the least I could do. We needed answers. *I* needed answers. Who better than me to interact with the people who dwelled so much in darkness? Thor or Loki they'd have seen as an immediate threat. Baldur... I didn't think he'd have had any idea where to begin. And I wasn't going to ask any more of Ari, not when she'd already shouldered so many burdens that weren't meant to be hers.

She'd asked us to look beyond the obvious. I might not be able to see, but I could still do that much for the woman I loved.

I didn't need vision now. I was the Allfather's son, and his blood sang through my veins. The branches of the great tree resonated at different frequencies as I passed them, leaving a faint aftertaste on my tongue. A hint of grass and soil that was Midgard. The floral sweetness of Vanaheim, Freya's former home. A salty chill I knew was Niflheim, the realm of ice. And then a damp mossy impression that could belong only to Nidavellir, home of the dark elves.

I tested the branch with my feet and then walked cautiously along it. A quiver of energy emanated from the gate at its end. I paused there for a moment, dragging in a breath, gathering strands of shadow around me like a shield. Then I strode into the gate's embrace.

The air contracted around me, and a second later my boots hit uneven stone. A cool dampness congealed against my skin. Only the faintest current stirred the air around me. I reached out one hand, and it found a rough rocky wall just a couple of feet to my left.

The gate still quavered behind me. As long as I stayed where I was, I should be able to step right back into it when I needed to.

I wasn't alone. In the moment it took me to get my bearings, a shoe scuffed against the stone floor somewhere not far ahead of me. There was a faint rasp of breath. The air shifted minutely against my skin. They were gesturing to each other, I thought. Maybe still concealed in dark alcoves that would had hid them from anyone relying on sight.

The dark elves had fallen on Ari when she'd come this way looking for Odin. They'd slaughtered the three valkyries who'd come before her, from what she'd said of the vision Muninn had shown her as a threat. But attempting to kill a god was an entirely different matter. I might not have been able to offer much of an offensive on my own, but with my shadowy magic and the gate at my back, these mortal creatures weren't likely to hurt me either.

People, I reminded myself. Not creatures. They might have thrown themselves at us like animals more than once in the last few weeks, but they still had far more reason than a warg or a draug did. I wouldn't have come otherwise.

"What are you doing here, god of Asgard?" a sharp voice called out when I didn't move. "We have nothing of yours."

I turned my head toward the sound in as close a semblance of meeting the speaker's eyes as I could manage. "I'm not here to take or to attack," I said. "I'm here to learn. Who do you answer to? I'd like to speak to them."

Murmurs passed between the gate's guards—in the tongue of the dark elves, but I'd studied enough languages in my reading to recognize the words for *blind one*. They'd identified me. Good. That should work in my favor. Make me seem even less a reason for concern.

"Why should he come to you?" asked a different voice, this one female. "Maybe your friends are waiting on the other side of that gate to burst through."

"If we wanted to launch an assault, don't you think there'd be easier ways?" I said.

"You expect us to trust you an awful lot when you don't trust us at all," she retorted. The others muttered in agreement.

They might have a point. Simply arriving here braced for an attack wasn't all that great a show of good faith. My chest constricted, but I nodded. I'd come this far—I'd see my private mission through.

"I'll come with you to a meeting spot farther from the gate," I said. "But we will go slowly, and we will not go far. I'm already on your ground here."

More muttering, this round so low I couldn't make out the words at all. The man who'd spoken first let out a huff.

"Come," he said. "Then we'll see if the commander will meet you."

One of them touched my arm. I managed to detach it gently rather than yanking it away as I'd wanted to. "You walk," I said. "I can follow you well enough." I'd keep a better sense of space if I was navigating by my own powers.

I extended a length of shadow like a cane and treaded after the two guards who were leading me. My back prickled with the awareness of the few we were leaving behind. Technically I was now surrounded.

Between my free hand following the wall and the shadow cane testing the space around me, I formed a mental map in my head as I followed the scrape of the dark elves' feet. The tunnel curved to the left. We passed another cave opening at our right with a waft of slightly warmer air. After about five minutes, my guides stopped in a space that felt about the size of the dining room in my hall back in Asgard. My shadows flicked across walls sloping up toward a high ceiling.

"Wait here," the man said. The woman stayed, leaning against the wall with a rustle of her clothes, as he hustled off. I stood still and straight, fighting the impression that I might be making a horrendous mistake.

It seemed a long while that I waited. My mouth grew dry, my shoulders stiff from standing at attention. Then several sets of footsteps sounded in the passage where the guard had disappeared. The clink of metal reached my ears.

The commander had brought more guards. I had to hope they were intended for his protection and not to try to capture me.

They drew to a stop at the mouth of the passage. I suspected he hadn't even entered the room. His gravelly voice carried across the room to me.

"You wanted to speak to someone in charge. Here I

am. I can't speak for all the dark elves, but I'm the best you're going to get. What do you want, god of darkness?"

I found I didn't know what to say other than the truth. Maybe Loki would have had some sly way of getting at the subject he wanted, but I didn't see much point in beating around the bush. Mostly I wanted to be done with this and gone from here, back to the open warmth and fresh winds of Asgard.

"I want to know why you've allied with Surt against us," I said. "Why you've been killing humans for him. Why you helped him capture Odin."

The commander let out a hoarse laugh. "And you figure I should tell you just because you asked?"

"I think something must have gone wrong. This kind of violence hasn't been the way of the dark elves in the past."

"'Gone wrong,'" he repeated, with what sounded like a shake of his head. "And you have no idea. This is what it takes to bring you to our doorstep. What are you even offering if I tell you there is something wrong?"

"Perhaps we could help you set things right," I said. "In a way that doesn't require debasing yourself for that monster."

"Monster?" the commander scoffed. "The giant is the only one who's stood up to fight for our survival. While you and your fellow Asgardians lounge around enjoying your lovely city, forgetting the rest of us even exist."

My jaw clenched. "I'm here *now*. I'm listening now. Whether you take this chance is up to *you*. If the gods 'forget' you after this, you'll have no one to blame but yourself."

"Oh, so this is one more way to wash your hands of us, then? I'm not sure I even believe you don't know. Your great Odin was down here to witness the state of things for himself. And doesn't he see all when he looks down over the realms. But what has he ever cared for anyone but his own?"

The last words rang with bitterness so pungent it seemed to sear right through my skin. Right down to the smoldering anger I'd tamped down earlier. Before I'd thought through my response, it had already tumbled out.

"What makes you think he cares about even his own all that much?"

The commander paused for a moment. "Strange words from one of those who was very anxious to get him back."

He sounded skeptical, but there was something more open in his tone now. Something curious. I barreled onward.

"You know who I am, don't you? You know my story. You know who ordered my first death. I saved him, yes. That doesn't mean I'd defend his every action. I'm here *because* I don't trust every act he takes. Whatever's happened, whatever he might know about your complaints, he hasn't shared that with the rest of us. I swear to you, I want to know even if he doesn't."

Silence hung between us. When the commander spoke again, his voice was raw.

"I still say you're hundreds of years too late. That's how long it's been since the caves started collapsing. Should I tell you how much smaller our realm has become as the rock grows more brittle? How many have died with the ceiling of their homes crashing down over their heads? How the gardens we once maintained have begun to shrivel with rot? What it's like to hear the sobbing of children who are hungry or ill or homeless every day of your life?"

A wave of horror rolled over me. "I didn't know," I said.

"Of course you didn't. Why would you think about things like that off in your fancy halls where all is well? We made you your weapons and your armor for your war, and then when the end was over, what use did you have for us? When have any of your kind set foot in our realm of their own accord since Ragnarok?"

He stepped back with the tap of a spear-end against the rock floor. "We haven't lowered ourselves to anything. The world we live in brought us low. We're just trying to claw our way back up. When it's that or watch your people die, I wonder if you'd really choose any differently. Take *that* back to Asgard, Blind One."

12

Aria

In that first early hour after I woke up, when Asgard was quiet and the sun just rising over the majestic buildings, I could almost forget we were on the verge of war. I stopped outside my hall, soaking in the dawn light. Then I spotted a golden falcon plummeting from the sky.

My heart lurched. That was Freya's falcon form. Had she been on the patrol just now—had she seen something?

I hurried over, reaching her just as her feet touched the tiles outside her own gleaming hall. She shook off the falcon cloak with a swish of the golden hair it matched and swiped her hand across her eyes. She looked tired. The impression didn't detract from her beautiful face at all, but it was unnerving to see all the same.

"What happened?" I asked. "Is Surt making another attack? Do we need to wake everyone up?"

Freya turned her blue eyes toward me, blinking for a second as if she'd forgotten that anyone else might be around. She rolled her shoulders with a twist of her mouth that didn't quite make it into a smile.

"No attack," she said. "No sign of Surt. I was out searching for Hnoss—for my daughter."

"Oh." From her expression, she hadn't found the younger goddess. I groped for something to say. "I guess there must be a lot of places to look."

"Yes," Freya agreed. "And I've been to all of the ones I can think of. It's been so long... It's hard to say how her tastes might have changed. I suppose I don't even know for sure she's there to be found."

Her voice wobbled, just slightly but enough to make my throat close up. What would I have done if Petey had been lost to me, not only mentally but completely?

"I'm sure you'll find her eventually," I said. "You'd know if something had happened to her, wouldn't you? You must have the same kind of connection to her that told you and Thor and the others that Odin was still alive."

"Yes," she said. "As vague as that is." Her jaw twitched. She smothered a yawn. Had she been out flying all night? "I'd appreciate that more if it would lead me to her."

"It's something," I said. What I wouldn't have given for a tie like that to Petey.

It seemed insensitive to say anything like that, but Freya's gaze turned knowing. The pain this conversation had stirred up in me must have shown on my face—or maybe she could sense it in other ways. She'd told me once that being the goddess of love didn't only mean the romantic kind but all sorts. And if I loved anyone, it was Petey.

"I'm sorry," she said. "I wasn't thinking of how hard it must be for you to be separated from your brother, with the things that have been happening on Midgard. You could look in on him, couldn't you?"

"Not on my own," I said. "That's how the dark elves found out about him in the first place." Even if I'd asked Loki to take me to watch Petey for a few moments hidden by his sly magic, I wasn't sure that would make anything easier. I couldn't stay to protect him. It would only distract me from what I needed to do here.

It'd be selfish, asking for that, taking that time and energy just to comfort myself for a minute or two. When we'd stopped Surt, when we knew he wasn't a threat anymore, then I could go without risking Petey more.

Freya lifted her head at the sound of footsteps. Odin was walking toward us, slow and steady, his posture a little less imperious than usual. When he reached us, he set his hand gently on the small of Freya's back and inclined his head toward her. "Wife."

"Husband," she said in a wry tone, the corner of her mouth curling up. I'd never quite wrapped my head around the idea that the two of them were a couple, but seeing that brief intimacy between them made it suddenly real.

I might have had a lot of beefs with Odin, but I could feel in that moment without even trying that he cared about his wife.

"We were just discussing little ones beyond our reach," Freya said. "Although I suppose it's a bit much to call Hnoss 'little' at this point. You haven't seen any sign of her in your glimpses from on high, have you?"

The Allfather shook his head. "I would tell you as soon as I did."

Would he? I wasn't sure I believed *that*, no matter how soft his gaze had become as he looked at her. Mostly because a flinty gleam came back into his eyes the second they shifted toward me.

To be fair, we hadn't exactly ended our last serious conversation on a positive note.

"You look in from time to time on Aria's brother, too, don't you?" Freya said.

Odin's gaze stayed on me. "Is that what's weighing on the valkyrie? Surt and his minions have not ventured near him."

Yeah, I definitely didn't trust him to tell me if I had something to worry about there. He wanted me practicing with the gods and honing our powers, not fretting about mortals. "Good to know," I said with forced cheer.

"If it would ease your mind," he went in on his impenetrable voice, "I could let you see for yourself."

I would have thought I was prepared for anything he could have said, but that offer left me speechless. Freya blinked at him with unmistakable surprise of her own.

"From—from your seat, up there?" I checked, waving my hand toward his hall at the end of the road.

"Where else?"

"I thought you didn't let anyone up there."

Odin smiled a thin and equally impenetrable smile. "You are a special case, are you not? A valkyrie I had no hand in creating, who was never prepared to venture onto a battlefield. And yet it's through you that my sons and blood-sworn brother have found an even greater strength. If it will keep you from distraction later when it matters most, making a small exception is very little price to pay."

He had made exceptions before, hadn't he? He'd brought Loki there for their secret meetings about Odin's dark plans. A fact which didn't exactly reassure me. But Freya was nodding now, her own smile growing, as if she thought his offer was a delightful idea.

"You can see him without Surt's fiends ever knowing," she said. "You deserve that, after everything you've given up for us."

I hadn't realized she'd considered how much I'd given up in any detail. Trading Midgard for Asgard must have seemed like a huge step up to her. But maybe all that time worrying about her daughter had gotten her thinking about the many different factors that went into making a place a real home.

Odin was watching me, waiting. What would he make of it if I said no? Was that even a reasonable choice? I *did* want to see Petey, with every fiber of my being.

"All right," I said. "Can we go now?"

The Allfather turned with a flap of his great cloak and a beckoning gesture. He strode back toward his hall without checking to see if I was following. I hurried after him, tempted to unfurl my wings and show I could make it there faster than him if I really wanted to.

We went through his hall, past the front room where the group of us had paid our respects before and on into the silent depths between the stone walls. Odin turned through a doorway into a small room that held nothing but a ladder with thick oak rungs. A circular panel covered the ceiling above it. He climbed the ladder, pressed a few points on the panel too quickly for me to follow the movement, and slid it aside. With a short huff of breath, he vanished through the opening.

My heart thumped faster as I clambered after him. I crawled out onto the hardwood floor of an unsettlingly familiar room. Tall windows loomed in a ring around me beneath a high peaked ceiling. A tall wooden chair stood in their midst—a larger and more worn version of the throne-like seat he had in his meeting room below. The whole space smelled like the ozone after a storm.

I was rather intimately familiar with that chair, or at least the construct of it Muninn had brought into being. I'd leaned against it while Loki's lips and tongue had sent waves of pleasure through my core. I'd perched on one of those broad wooden arms with Thor inside me. The memories sparked a tingle between my legs and brought a flush to my cheeks.

Odin couldn't know about any of *that*, I was pretty sure. He'd been stuck in a cage in a cave in Muspelheim when it had happened. And it hadn't really been this room or this chair. Better to put all that out of my mind.

"How does it work?" I asked, setting my hand on the side of the chair. The wood was surprisingly warm.

"Sit," Odin said, tipping his head. "Settle in. You'll see better if you're comfortable."

Ah, yeah, I was not going to feel super comfortable as long as I was in this room with the Allfather. But I gave it my best shot, scrambling onto the smooth seat and shoving myself so I could lean against the back of it. My feet would have dangled like a little kid's, so I tucked them into a cross-legged position instead. My hands came to rest instinctively on the arms of the chair.

"Each of the windows looks out onto a realm," Odin said beside me. "Can you tell which one is Midgard?"

I studied each of the ones I could see in turn. Symbols I hadn't noticed before were carved into the stone above each window. That one, like a flame, was obviously Muspelheim. My gaze settled on one at my other side, a tree-like symbol that tugged at me. I pointed. "There."

"Well done, valkyrie." Odin nudged the chair, and it glided around to face that window. The view beyond the frame was hazy. As I squinted at it, trying to bring something into focus, a rushing sensation crept over me, as if a sharp breeze were blowing under my skin instead of over it. My breath caught at the base of my throat.

"Let yourself go," the Allfather said in a low voice. "I'll help you find your way." He touched my shoulder, his fingers settling into place with a steadying grip.

My pulse hammered even harder, but I gave myself over to the rushing sensation. Petey was out there somewhere. This feeling would take me to him.

The landscape beyond the window spiraled with flashes of color. My sense of the room around me faded away as if the window had drawn me to it, though I could still feel the hard surface of the chair beneath me. Lakes and hills and buildings whipped by, until my stomach churned with dizziness. Then the view jerked to a halt looking down over a small backyard surrounded by an actual white picket fence.

A boy was sitting at a patio table on the low deck, the sun gleaming in his blond hair, his hand clutched around a spoon he was digging into his cereal bowl. Petey. A gasp escaped me. He was right there, and so real—

The woman sitting across from him—his foster mother—gave him a soft smile as he scooped up the last of his breakfast. "Would you like any more, honey?" she asked.

"No, thank you," Petey said in his shyly sweet voice, but he smiled back. His blue-gray eyes shifted to the cereal box. He reached out and grazed his fingers over an image there. I peered closer.

It was a photograph of one of the trading cards he collected. The kind I'd always been sneaking him packs of when I'd figured our mom wouldn't notice. His brow knit as he looked at it, and my gut twisted.

"We already got the prize out when we first opened the box. Remember?" His foster mother got up, taking his bowl, and ruffled his hair with clear affection. "There'll be another one in the next box."

"I know," Petey said, but his expression stayed pensive. Confused. How much could he even remember after Hod had wiped me and the rest of the people he'd known from his mind? Did he know he'd used to have a big set of them, fat enough that he'd needed two rubber bands to hold them in place? Did he have a sense that *someone* had pored over them with him and brought new ones for him to unwrap?

He got up and went down the deck's single step onto the trimmed lawn. A plastic tub of toys sat next to the step. He grabbed a couple of plastic dinosaur figurines and started them marching into the grass that came up to their bellies. After a minute, he paused, looking down the lawn as if he expected a playmate to come join him.

This one's a triceratops, so we'll call her Sera. I think she's best friends with your stegosaurus.

Of course she is. My toys are always best friends with yours, Ari. They get lonely when you can't come and see us.

I know, kiddo. I know. Soon, you'll get to see me all the time. I promise.

God, how many times had I made promises like that? Promises there was no way in hell I could keep now. Heat built up behind my eyes.

At the same moment, Petey's chin wobbled.

"Why did you leave me all alone?" he whispered to whatever vague shapes of memories he had of times before.

A sob choked me, and the scene in the backyard hurtled away. I slammed into the back of the chair so hard a jolt of pain shot up my spine. But it was nothing compared to the ache clutching my chest.

"Let me see him again," I sputtered. "I need to—I have to—"

"I think you've seen enough," Odin said, in a voice that wasn't quite gentle but wasn't accusing either. "He's safe. He's well looked-after. Isn't that what was important to you?"

My hands clenched against the arms of the chair. "Yes," I had to say. It was.

I'd also wanted him to be happy. He was away from Mom and her ranting and neglect. He was away from her boyfriends with their bruising hands.

But he'd looked so fucking *sad*.

13

Aria

The shakes started before I'd made it out of Odin's room with the ladder. I managed to hold myself stiffly in control as the Allfather showed me out of his hall. I couldn't tell what reaction he'd been looking for in me, but I'd be damned if he saw me break down.

I stepped out onto the marble tiles, and a tremor crept across my shoulders. I spun and hurried around Odin's hall, past the few smaller ones that were no longer occupied along the edge of the city, and into the narrow strip of forest that stretched between the city and the apple orchard that had once granted the gods their immortality.

When the trees had closed around me, I sank down to the ground with my back against a pine. A bird fluttered past through the soft warmth of the morning, and the scent of green growing things filled my lungs. None of it was enough to settle my nerves. I buried my face in my hands and breathed with a rasp, sucking air past my palms. My whole body shuddered.

Get it together, Ari. You've been through worse. So much worse.

But I couldn't erase Petey's thin voice from my memory. That plaintive question, that he couldn't even have known who he was asking. All he knew was *someone* had left him behind, without any ties to the life he'd had before.

I'm sorry, I thought at him, as if there was any chance he'd hear me. *I'm so fucking sorry.*

Even grappling with my tangled feelings, I didn't miss the crunch of footsteps approaching. My head jerked up, my body tensing. I forced it to relax as much as I could manage, grateful that no actual tears had slipped out to redden my eyes.

Loki ambled between the trees. He'd picked a deep purple tunic this morning, one that made his ivory skin look even paler and his hair flame even brighter. For about half a second I hoped he'd just been going for a stroll and he might not even notice me, but then he met my gaze so nonchalantly I knew he'd come out this way specifically to find me.

He meandered the rest of the way over and propped himself against the ash tree opposite my pine. "Ari," he said with a nod of greeting. His tone was light, but his eyes were searching.

"Loki," I replied. Despite my best efforts, my voice creaked a little. The strain of too much withheld emotion.

"You paid a visit to the Allfather, I noticed," he remarked.

My hackles rose instinctively. "I thought you said you weren't tracking my every move."

He gave me a baleful look. "Why do you assume I was monitoring *you*?"

Oh. He'd been keeping an eye on all of the comings and goings at Odin's hall? I couldn't really blame him for that, considering what the king of the gods had put him through.

"He offered to let me see Petey from his seat," I said. "I haven't, not for real, since we left him with the foster family. It was a way to check in on him without throwing off our plans or putting him in danger..."

I hadn't realized how tight Loki's expression was until it softened. "Oh, pixie," he said. "Of course you had to see." He cocked his head. "What happened? If he *had* been in danger, you'd already be halfway across Midgard to save him. But you hardly look pleased."

I rubbed my temples. "I don't know what I was expecting. Somehow I thought he could just move on from the blank slate we left him with. But he knows he's missing something. How could he not? We left a huge black hole in his memory. And it's weighing on him. I could see that."

"What did Odin make of all that?"

"I don't know." I threw my hands in the air. "What does he make of anything? He just told me that I should be glad Petey's safe and not to dwell on it or something. He didn't seem concerned, if that's what you mean."

"No. Of course he didn't." Loki let out a ragged

laugh, and I realized his stance had gone rigid again. "That's how he always likes us," he went on in a distant voice that barely sounded as if it were directed at me. "Dangling over a precipice. Never quite on solid ground." His mouth closed with a snap. His amber eyes glimmered with a sudden spark. He held out his hand to me. "Come with me."

"What?" I said, easing myself onto my feet. "Where?"

"Just come." He grasped my fingers and tugged me into his arms. The next thing I knew, he'd taken off into the air with me braced against him, my head by his shoulder, my hip against his waist.

I had to loop my arm around the back of his neck to hold myself steady as the ground whipped by beneath us. "Loki! What are you doing?"

"Refusing to stand down," he muttered, whatever that was supposed to mean. The lean muscles in his arms were flexed hard where they were wrapped around me. His eyes were still blazing, his mouth set in a grim line as we soared onward, as much creating the wind as chasing it. The sharp heat of his fiery power seeped from his body into mine. I wasn't sure anything short of an incoming jumbo jet could have thrown him off course, and maybe not even that.

Sometimes I could almost forget I was dealing with gods. Not now. All I could do was cling on and see where we ended up.

We raced over the rainbow bridge and across the land below, passing over the terrain so quickly I couldn't make out more than a blur. It wasn't that long before Loki slowed. He came to an abrupt halt but landed with his usual grace on a rooftop on a residential street.

A familiar rooftop. A familiar street. I'd perched here with Hod to watch Loki and Baldur escort Petey into his new home: that two-story house with light blue clapboard I was staring at right now. He might still be playing with his dinosaurs in the backyard. It couldn't have been more than an hour since I'd seen him from Odin's high seat.

My stomach flipped over, and my legs wobbled under me as the trickster set me down. "Loki?"

"No one can see us," he said. "Not a single dark elf eye will make us out. But if you want, we can let your brother see you. You can tell him—whatever you like. Whatever you need to. Be there for him. Damn the rest."

My jaw dropped. I turned from Loki to the house, a queasy sensation uncoiling in my gut.

I'd thought about asking him to bring me here, concealed, so many times. I'd dreamed about walking back into Petey's life. The longing shot through my heart with a painful throb.

I took a step toward the edge of the roof, and my stomach churned harder. I swallowed thickly. The longing was there, but so were all the reasons I'd had to hesitate.

"I can't," I said. "I hate what we did to him, but I hate what could have happened to him if we hadn't even more. It's better... It's better that he be sad than be dead. He'll get past it. It's only been a week." He'd get past me, the me he couldn't remember, in time. A fresh lump rose in my throat. "I have to do what's best for him, and what's best for him is putting all my energy into stopping Surt."

Loki slid his arm around my shoulders. The almost manic urgency that had seemed to be driving him earlier had dissipated. I couldn't help leaning into him, letting him take some of my weight. My whole body abruptly felt very heavy.

"And they thought the valkyrie I'd bring them wouldn't be noble," he muttered.

I made a dismissive sound. "You picked someone like you, didn't you? How many times did you ignore what *you* wanted for what you thought was the greater good?"

That hoarse laugh escaped him again. "Maybe I was trying to rewrite a little of that history today." He stroked his thumb up and down the side of my arm. "Are you sure?"

The word caught in my throat for a second, but I knew what I had to say. "Yeah. I'm sure."

He bowed his head toward mine, his lips grazing my forehead. "Do you mind if I show you something else, while we're down here?"

"Of course not. What is it?"

"It'll be easier to explain when we're there."

I let him heft me up piggyback-style this time, now that I had more choice in the matter. The trickster god set off at a somewhat less frantic pace, but the city fell away behind us in the space of a few beats of my heart. Loki sped on, over fields and forests, towns and more cities, until a broad expanse of shimmering blue came into view ahead of us.

The trickster came to earth on a rocky beach. We were immediately buffeted by a wet salty wind. There was no one else in sight, just us and the gray stones and the paler gray of the ocean.

"You know I can change my shape," Loki said after a moment of silence.

"You demonstrated that very vividly the first day we met," I said, remembering the way he'd shifted his face to look like a woman's. Since then I'd also seen him transform into a wolf nearly big enough to rival the wargs we'd battled.

He nodded. "It seems because of that... when I have children, they don't always turn out quite as you'd expect."

I glanced at him. "How do they turn out?"

He gazed across the sea for a minute, his expression as serious as I'd ever seen him. "I had another wife, a giant wife, before my wife in Asgard—ages ago. She gave me three children. One of them, the girl, looked human enough, but deathly-dark all down one side. My sons came in the form of a wolf and a serpent. All of them as aware and intelligent as you or me, mind you."

I'd seen enough craziness in the last month to take that information in stride. "Where are they now?" I asked, thinking of Freya's quest to find her daughter.

"My daughter, you could say, was the lucky one," Loki said. "The gods couldn't stand the sight of her, so Odin cast her down to the realm of the dead, to oversee the souls who find themselves there."

He swiped his hand across his mouth, his voice going carefully flat. "My sons died in Ragnarok. Attacking the gods by my side. They weren't really monsters, you know. But that was how Asgard saw them, how Asgard treated them... They chained up Fenrir, the wolf, and kept him prisoner. And Jormungandr, the serpent, they hurled into this ocean on pain of death should he emerge. A promise Thor saw through when the time came."

I winced. "I'm sorry," I said. How much of his children's torments had Muninn taunted him with?

I turned to him, hugging him. Loki tipped my face up with a brush of his fingers over my jaw, and I welcomed his kiss. With the chilly wind whipping around us, for a moment it felt as if he were the only warmth in the whole world.

When I drew back, he was smiling. "It's all ancient history now, as they say," he said, his usual flippant tone returning. "I'm told it builds character to remind oneself of sacrifices made and pains endured."

No, he'd brought me out here for more than that. "Are you okay?" I asked.

He dismissed the question with a flick of his finger. "My dear Ari, when am I ever anything else? Come on now, I've had my fill of playing the maudlin for today. You want to defeat Surt? We'd best get back to our training before the others sound the alarm."

He scooped me onto his back easily, and I rested my head against his neck as he leapt up toward the sky. My gut was knotted tight. He'd snapped himself out of his melancholy, but I didn't believe for a second that the "ancient history" he'd talked about didn't haunt him.

If this was the message he'd wanted to convey to me, he could consider it received: It'd be over my dead body before Petey faced even a fragment of what Odin's scheming had done to Loki and his children.

14

Baldur

I was halfway to the practice field when my father's path converged with mine. I glanced at Odin as he fell into step beside me. His cloak looked even more faded than usual, the peak of his hat more crumpled, but his brown eye gleamed brightly.

"My son," he said with the warmth he always offered me. I'd never really thought before about the fact that he didn't use the same tone with everyone. Not even with my twin. But now, after the raw conversations Hod and I had been propelled into, the difference niggled at me. Why should I get that preferential treatment?

"Father," I replied with a dip of my head.

"How do you feel your training is coming along?" he asked. "This joint power the four of you have found, is it coalescing?"

"Five," I said automatically. "The five of us."

"The valkyrie. Yes. Although it seems she is more of a conduit than a force in herself."

I choked on a laugh. He wouldn't have said that if he'd ever seen Aria in real action. "She might not have godly strength or magic," I said, "but she's a fighter to be reckoned with. She's had much less time than the rest of us to stretch her powers."

Odin hummed to himself. A skeptical sound. Part of me wanted to insist he give Aria her due respect, and another part balked. Deserved or not, I had my father's favor. Did I really want to find out what it might be like to lose it?

Of course, even with his favor, he'd let me die and linger for ages in that void, as part of the grand plan he'd never bothered to share with the rest of us. A ripple of shadow passed through me, bleeding tendrils from my fingertips. I swiped them away against my shirt, feeling the threads fray in their wake.

This wasn't the time for bringing up all that history. Not when the giant who'd once slaughtered so many of us meant to repeat the job. I brought my mind back to Odin's question.

"I think the cohesion between us is becoming more instinctive," I said. "For now we've been relying on one of us—usually Thor—giving our cue to move in unison, but the moments of natural harmony are coming more frequently. Freya has been providing some 'surprise' elements to keep us on our toes."

My father chuckled. "I can imagine she's enjoying that. From what I've gathered, you handled your last encounter with the dark elves well. Do you think you'd soon be ready to confront a larger foe?"

Our last encounter with the dark elves, when we'd sealed the second gate on Midgard, had felt far too easy. Less like a battle and more like an extermination. The shadows seeping from behind my ribs twitched. Every day, more of them wriggled free, searing through the light that normally filled my chest.

"It's difficult to say," I said. "Do you think we need to take the battle to Surt already? We've hindered his supply of draugr soldiers. I'm not sure it'd be wise to launch an offensive on his home ground until our combined powers are completely in sync." And perhaps not even then. The five of us—seven, if Freya and Odin joined the fight as well—against the giant of flames and his entire army in the realm he'd claimed as his own? Surely we needed more preparation before we attempted that.

"The longer he remains active, the greater the scourge," Odin murmured in his vague way. "Well, I will see your progress for myself, I think."

The others were already standing in the practice area where the field's grass was alternately trampled, gouged, and burnt from our previous efforts. Several physical targets stood at various points around our group, but after the number we'd destroyed, Freya had taken to conjuring the illusion of other attackers around those with her magic. "More fighting, less crafting," she'd said yesterday.

Odin halted at the edge of the field as I loped over to join my companions. Thor and Loki were talking, Thor letting out a bellow of laughter at something the trickster had said. Aria shot me a welcoming smile. My twin smiled too, but Hod's eyes stayed dark. I studied him, wondering if he looked grimmer than usual or if I'd simply become more affected by his moods now that I wasn't wrapping myself in a gauze of dreaminess to escape anything that might provoke distress.

"The gang's all here now," Freya called from the sidelines. "Shall we get started?"

The truth was that despite my hesitation with my father, the style of combat we'd been discovering between the five of us was becoming second nature. My gaze caught Thor's and then Loki's as Aria took her position in our midst. A tingle of connection passed over my skin from every direction. I felt as much as heard our breaths fall into rhythm with each other, our movements start to sync up without any conscious effort.

It was becoming natural here on the practice field where we'd worked on that harmony so much. How organically would we slide into these patterns with an army of draugr coming at us?

Hod came up beside me, and along with the sense of our unified connection, a shudder of tension wafted off of him. I frowned. Something was bothering him, clearly. He was trying to stand loosely, but that tension was wound through the muscles of his shoulders and down his back. Was it only having our father here watching us that had affected him? He might not be able to see Odin, but I had no doubt he'd picked up the Allfather's voice as we'd approached.

I could hardly ask him about that with Odin right there to overhear. Later I could offer my ear, if he wanted to talk. It was the least I could offer after how long I'd spent avoiding any of the conversations that might have given him a little more peace.

We arranged ourselves before the first target. Freya's conjured figures wavered into being around it, a swarm of filmy dark elves. Thor raised his hammer as our signal, and we all leapt forward.

I never knew quite how the light I cast out would twine with the others. Our magic seemed to find its way of its own accord. This time it collided with Loki's slash of fire, sparking the flames brighter and hotter. Thor's hammer flew through them, sending them even higher with a crackle of lightning and emerging with a glowing blaze to smash into the one solid target. The illusionary figures hissed out of existence in the wake of the flames.

Freya wasn't done yet. I'd only just registered our "victory" when several bolts of magic screamed down at us from above. We whipped around with a common heartbeat. A flash of lightning burst from Aria's hands, smaller than Thor's but still potent. I hurled a blazing glow upward in unison with the others and watched those beams spin around Hod's shadowy missile before both split apart to shatter through our "attackers."

The torn strands of Freya's magic dispelled as they cascaded harmlessly down. Thor let out a triumphant shout and raised his hand for a high five that Aria jumped up to return. From across the field, Odin applauded us with a slow clap.

"This is how we'll defeat those villains," he said in a pleased voice. "See how much farther you can hone that power."

He turned to meander off again, and Freya picked that moment to hurl a couple of the other straw targets our way. I flinched and spun at the rustling, the others jerking around in turn.

Thor's shout to direct us was more instinctive than calculated, but it served as a cue all the same. We blasted the targets together. Singed straw rained down over us.

"Villains," Hod repeated under his breath as he swiped at a few shreds of straw that had clung to his shirt. He turned his head the way Odin had gone, cocking it as if listening. Our father had already disappeared between the city's buildings.

"He's gone," Aria said. "What's bothering you?"

Hod's jaw set. He swiveled back to face the rest of us. "I went down to Nidavellir to talk to the dark elves this morning."

"What?" Thor exclaimed, and Aria's eyes widened.

Loki's eyebrows arched. "So, Mr. Doom and Gloom does have a few tricks up his sleeve."

Hod grimaced in the trickster's direction.

"What did you find out?" I asked, my chest tightening. It obviously wasn't anything *good*, from the way he was behaving.

"Oh, there's resentment there for sure," he said. "They didn't apologize for what they've been doing. But it didn't sound as if they were all that happy about the choices available to them either. The realms have become even more unstable than we might have thought. The caves of Nidavellir are crumbling. The dark elves barely able to grow enough food to sustain themselves. The situation for them is clearly 'Kill or die,' and I'm not sure I can blame them for taking the former route. Surt's the only one offering them any way out."

"Is there anything we *can* do?" Aria said.

Hod's head bowed. "I don't know. I don't know why the realms are failing at all. But if anyone does, it's Odin, and he's pretending he doesn't know a thing about it. He must have some idea. We brought the matter up with him directly, and he acted as if they had no reason other than spite."

He bit off the last word, his stance tensing even more. The darkness twisted through my innards spasmed.

My hands clenched against that chilling sensation. A fragment tumbled from my fingers anyway, dappling the grass at my feet with rot. My heart lurched, but everyone's attention was still fixed on Hod.

"If he knew—" Freya started.

Hod lifted his head toward her. "Do you honestly think there's any way he doesn't?"

Her voice faltered. She pulled her posture up straighter. "I'll speak to him. I don't need to tell him that you went behind his back. I can simply urge him to consider other possibilities, to dig deeper, to be open at least with me."

And we'd see how far that got us. A sudden sense of hopelessness pierced my chest. What could we accomplish when even the one who should be guiding us might be leading us astray?

"We should finish our training," I heard myself saying without having thought through the words. "We're all set up now, and we will still need to fight. Then—then we can discuss how to proceed."

"I'll agree with that," Thor said gruffly, which seemed to settle things. We shifted, a little more begrudgingly than before, toward the next target. Freya bit her lip and motioned with her arm to summon forth more of her magic. Not dark elves this time. Draugr.

The sight of their bloated bodies, even hazy as the conjured forms were, dredged up a wrenching memory from Muninn's prison: that moment when Hod and I had knelt by my own slumped body, and it had risen like a draug itself, accusing my twin with every dark thought I'd tried to burn away.

Thor gave a shout. We all lunged forward. I whipped out a scorching bolt of light—and the dark tendrils inside me wrenched out with it. The blaze stuck the target as I'd intended, but as it flew it flung the dark mass to the side. The tendrils smacked into Loki's calf with a searing hiss.

The trickster yelped and fell back on his ass as he pawed at the clotted energy clinging to him. Blood was already seeping through the leg of his slacks. My pulse stuttering, I threw myself to him, summoning healing light into my shaking hands.

"What in the nine realms was that about, Freya?" Loki sputtered. "*I'm* not the sodding target."

My shoulders stiffened, but I knew it was too late now. I couldn't hide this any longer.

"It wasn't Freya," I said as my magic melted away the trickster's wound and the vicious energy that had dealt it. "It was me. I didn't mean to—it slipped out before I could catch it."

Everyone was staring at me now, including Loki. "If you're covering for someone, that's a poor show," he said.

"That shadowy thing didn't look like anything that could have come from you. It could have been your twin's doing, though."

"No." I tipped back on my heels. The darkness inside me writhed even more insistently than it had before. It took no effort at all, when I wasn't fighting to suppress it, to raise my hand and let the tendrils seep from my palms.

"Baldur," Aria murmured.

"In my death," I said, before anyone had to ask. "In the void. It was dark and cold and—after a time it clawed its way into me. I thought I left it behind when I was reborn, but I never let myself look all that carefully. I— After Muninn— I can overcome it. I just have to find the right way."

I couldn't quite bring myself to look at any of them, not even my twin. So many threats before us, and I'd brought one right into our midst inside me.

15

Aria

Baldur looked so torn up that my chest constricted. I went to him, setting my hand on his shoulder where he was crouched next to Loki. "We'll figure it out," I said.

"Yes," Loki said, pushing himself to his feet and brushing himself off. "Perhaps we should hold off on further practice sessions until you've gotten that little hitch under control." He glanced at Freya. "You could have that chat with your husband."

Freya's mouth tightened, but she nodded.

"Do you need anything from the rest of us?" Thor asked his younger brother. "If I can help somehow—"

"No," Baldur said quietly. His voice had lost almost all of its usual brightness. "But thank you. It's in me. I'll see what I can do to better contain it."

Loki clapped Thor on the back. "Why don't you

come with me? I can think of a few other ways we might determine what's shaking up the realms. But people always seem to answer questions faster when you and your hammer are around."

There wasn't much humor in Thor's chuckle, but he followed Loki off the field. Hod knelt down at his twin's other side.

"What does it feel like?" he asked. "The darkness. Where is it coming from?"

"I'm not sure." Baldur touched the middle of his chest. "These cold strands of it just keep seeping out from somewhere inside me. They're too thick for my natural light to burn them away."

A thought struck me, so sudden and unnerving my throat closed up. "It isn't because—I encouraged you to explore other sides of yourself. To let yourself be wicked. Could that be why—"

Baldur was already shaking his head. He clasped my hand, lifting his bright blue eyes to meet my gaze. "This isn't your fault, Aria. Not at all. Whatever's in me, it's been there for a long time. I needed to face my past, and this is part of it. I just didn't realize there'd be so much of it, so deep, to overcome."

"And I doubt our father will be of much use," Hod muttered with a sharper edge than I usually heard from him. "For all we know, this is part of his great plan somehow."

The thrum of tension I'd felt from him earlier shivered over me. Baldur rubbed his forehead, his own expression taut. I groped for an idea to suggest, a course of action that gave me something to do other than walking away and leaving them to deal with this mess on their own.

"Maybe containing it isn't the right answer," I said, straightening up. "If you've got too much bottled up inside you, then why not let some out? You should be able to control it more if you're sending it out on purpose." I glanced over at the gleaming walls of Valhalla to the side of the field. "I get the feeling we might all enjoy blowing off some steam in a more concrete way."

Hod raised his eyebrows. "What did you have in mind, valkyrie?"

He'd used to call me that as if to distance himself from me. Now, the way he said the word sounded like a caress. A compliment that reminded me of all the powers I had in this new life I'd been given.

"It seems to me there are an awful lot of weapons in the hall of warriors that've been so sadly neglected," I said, allowing myself a smile. "What do you say we hack a few things up with our hands instead of all this magic here and magic there?"

Hod still looked skeptical, but he got up too. He offered his hand to his twin, who took it and pushed himself to his feet. We tramped across the field to Valhalla.

The swords and spears hanging on the walls glinted as ominously as they always had. I looked them over and settled on a short sword with a slightly curved blade and a leather-bound grip. The muscles in my arm flexed with my experimental swing. The sword wasn't as comfortable as my familiar switchblade, but it had a satisfying heft to it. Maybe it was time I moved on to more powerful weaponry.

Baldur detached a sword of his own, longer than the one I'd picked with a silver sheen that suited his natural light. It sang through the air when he gave it a whirl. For the first time since I'd seen him this morning, a hint of a smile curved his lips.

"I'm not sure giving the blind man sharp weaponry is the wisest idea," Hod said dryly. He ran his fingers tentatively over the blades mounted on the wall.

"We'll give you plenty of space," I said. There was a clear area in front of the hall's main doors, a span of some twenty feet before the rows of tables started. "If you feel like you want to do some hacking too."

"The idea *is* appealing. I'm thinking short would be better in this particular case." He tugged off a dagger that was only the length of his forearm and took a careful jab at the air in front of him. "I can give us something to fight, too."

At a wave of his other hand, shadows slipped across the floor and rose into blank human-like forms in front of each of us. Mine sidestepped when I did, following my movements.

"It'll stay with you," Hod said. "So I don't have to keep track of where you are. Do whatever you like to it. It's only shadow—you can't hurt it."

I swiped my sword through the figure's arm, and a wisp of darkness sloughed off with a hiss. Nice. I caught Baldur's eye, and he raised his own sword. His posture went rigid for a moment. Then a stream of darkness trickled from his palm down the blade.

I couldn't help watching as he lunged at the shadowy target. Something flashed in his eyes, fearful but determined. He cut straight through the figure's torso, the darkness he'd expelled coursing across the blade's path. The form shuddered, bits of shadow scattering the floor, and reconstructed itself.

Baldur swung the sword again and again, carving up the shadowy form with glints of steel and wafts of his own darkness. His expression became fiercer with each heft of the blade. A sheen of sweat formed on his forehead, dampening his white-blond hair. The emotions radiating off him were so fraught my heart started to ache.

He'd spent so long bottling up *everything* that had ever bothered him. I suspected it terrified him, letting any of that turmoil out. But what mattered to him most was making sure he never hurt any of us again, even by accident.

I turned back to my own target and gritted my teeth. *Slash.* That was for Odin and his secrets and his condescending tone. *Slash.* That was for Surt plotting to slaughter us all. *Slash.* That was for Muninn and the awful memories she'd thrown in our faces. The growing burn in my muscles brought a rush of relief.

A grunt across the room drew my attention. Despite his hesitation, Hod was tackling his own target, his feet planted in place in the section of the room he'd taken, several feet from Baldur and me. In the moment, my gaze found him, his expression was nothing but smoldering rage. He stabbed and wrenched his dagger through the shadows he could only have felt, not seen. His chest heaved with ragged breaths.

The ache around my heart squeezed tighter. I lowered my sword and set it on the top of the nearest table. Circling the benches, I came around to Hod's side of the room.

I was worried about startling him, but he must have heard the pad of my feet. He jabbed at his target a couple more times and then turned toward me. His face was flushed, his dark green eyes glittering with silent emotion.

"Are you all right?" I asked. I hadn't realized *he* might need the release quite this much.

He rotated the grip of the dagger in his hand as his jaw worked. "I'm fine," he said. "I've lasted this long under the Allfather's rule. I... I just don't know if I can protect *you* from whatever he might lead us into."

The ache turned into a lump that rose to my throat. "Hod..."

"This was good, though," he went on in a more casual tone, before I had to figure out what to say. "Let it out, like you said. I do feel more grounded. Is the sparring helping you, brother?"

Baldur had come to a stop at our voices. He nodded, wiping at the sweat on his forehead. "I think some of the darkness really is gone. It's less tangled up inside me right now—less twisted." He paused, and the corner of his mouth slanted down. "I wish I knew that it wouldn't come back. That this is all there is, and once I'm rid of it, I'm done."

That comment sent a different sort of twinge through me. It wasn't very long ago that I'd admitted to Loki how scared I'd become of the shadows inside *me*, the ones that could reach out through my body to claim lives as a valkyrie was supposed to. I'd managed to find a sort of peace with that power, hadn't I?

"Would it really be so bad if you couldn't get rid of all of it?" I said. "It doesn't have to hurt anyone. Hod carries darkness with him, and he decides how it acts." His shadows had proven they could bring pleasure just as easily as they could pain. The memory of them gliding over my skin sent a warmer shiver to my core. "You don't think of him any less for having it, do you?"

Baldur set down his sword, his mouth twisting but his gaze fond as he looked at his twin. "Of course not. But that's in his nature. It's simply a part of him. In me..."

"It isn't that different." A new urge came over me, with the release of some of that frustration I'd been carrying. I touched Hod's arm first, leaned in to brush my lips against his shoulder. His skin tasted faintly smoky. "And it's not a burden, something meant to be hidden away. It can be beautiful too." The next words wrenched a little coming out, a nervous tremor passing through my body, but I clamped down on that fear. "I love Hod's darkness."

Hod's voice came out thick with feeling. "Ari."

He cupped my face, and I gave myself over to his kiss. To everything he felt, dark and light, even if the tenderness of his touch stirred up enough longing in me to scare me. Then I moved from him to Baldur.

"I could love the darkness in you too."

The glow that came into the light god's eyes was nothing but hungry in that moment. His hand came to rest on my waist as I stepped right up to him, his breath hitching faintly as I pressed my mouth to his.

I soaked in the heat of his body against mine, the ripple of his muscles as his other arm came around me to pull me even closer. He angled his head to deepen the kiss, his tongue teasing over mine.

Desire flared low in my belly. I kissed the light god harder, running my hands up under his shirt to trace the lines of those muscles skin to skin. A groan escaped him.

He tipped my head back, and his mouth found the sensitive skin at the crook of my neck. His hands eased up my sides, spreading a shimmer of pleasure everywhere they touched. With a hoarse breath, he yanked off my tank top. A flick of his thumb loosened my bra.

Baldur brought his hand to my breast, a glow lighting on his palm. I whimpered as it tingled over my skin. A flicker of shadow joined it, a brief jolt of cold amid the heat. My nipple pebbled at the contrasting sensations. I didn't jerk away, but pushed into his touch encouragingly.

With a needy sound, he ducked his head to suck the tip of my breast into the wet heat of his mouth. I arched into him, a gasp slipping from my lips. But at the same time, my exposed skin prickled with the desire to be touched even more. To be encircled on both sides by this affection I'd never have dreamed I could have deserved.

Baldur worked my nipple over with his tongue, and I clutched the nape of his neck. I reached my other hand toward Hod. "Please. I want you more than witnessing today."

He moved to us so quickly I guessed I probably

hadn't needed the plea. The dark god's lips skimmed the side of my neck, his body pressing against me from behind. "Like this?" he murmured, his voice full of so much promise I all but quaked with longing.

"Yes. Oh!" His hand closed over my other breast, his thumb teasing the tip with another cool flicker of shadow. Baldur suckled me harder, and Hod turned my cheek so he could reach my mouth with his, and right then I was floating on nothing but pure bliss.

Bliss, and the burning for even more. Baldur's hand slipped down between my thighs. I cried out as he eased his fingers over my core through my jeans, spreading another warm glow flecked with chilly exhilaration in their wake. Hod released my mouth to kiss a path down my bare spine, and I tugged Baldur up to meet me for another kiss. My body rocked wantonly with the motion of his hand. My fingers trailed down his chest to the bulge behind the fly of his slacks.

He groaned again. I stroked him up and down, and a very specific wanting came over me.

I could do this. I wasn't a victim anymore. What I wanted, I could take—and give. The past didn't matter if I didn't let it.

My hand fumbled with the button and the zipper. Then I was tucking my fingers inside his loose boxers to circle the silky hard length of him. Baldur bucked into my gasp, his breath stuttering against my lips.

I pulled my mouth from his and wrenched up his shirt with my free hand. As I kept stroking him, I pressed kiss after kiss down the length of his torso. "Aria," he murmured when he must have realized where I was heading.

Hod sank onto his knees as I fell to mine. He fondled both of my breasts as he tested his teeth against my shoulder blade, right at the spot where my wings would have emerged.

A fresh wave of pleasure rolled through me. I swiped my tongue around Baldur's navel. Then I dipped my head and closed my lips around the head of his cock.

Baldur braced himself against the table behind him, his fingers tangling in my hair. I could feel him holding himself back from plunging deeper into my mouth. Every inch of him hummed with longing.

I slicked my tongue along the underside of his erection, drinking in the summer-sweet taste of him. As he shuddered, another hard length brushed my ass. Hod needed attention just as much as his brother. Hell, I was still burning to be filled between my legs as well as my mouth.

I shifted my ass back against him as I sucked Baldur down deeper. Hod nipped my back, and one hand dropped to the waist of my jeans. He trailed his fingers over my skin, tracing the hem of my panties, until I tugged his hand to my fly to show him I was all for this direction.

With a flutter of movement from his fingers and his shadows combined, he peeled my clothes down to my thighs. His fingertips circled my clit. I moaned around Baldur's cock, arching my back to give Hod better access.

He didn't need more of an invitation than that. With a rustle of his own clothes, his naked cock nudged between my legs. I gripped the base of Baldur's erection and gave him a firm pump as I edged my knees apart. Hod and I gasped together as he slid into me from behind.

Oh, Lord, yes, I loved this—being worshiped and worshiping in return. Hod moved inside me with smooth, steady thrusts, his mouth searing my neck, and I set a rhythm working my mouth and hand up and down Baldur's length. The light god's legs trembled as I took him even deeper.

"Fuck," he muttered, the first time I could remember hearing him swear. I took that as my cue to pick up the pace. His fingers tightened in my hair, holding me but not directing me. Letting me keep control the way I needed to. "Aria. I'm almost—I'm going to—"

He came with a rush of salty fluid and a wash of light that tingled from him through my entire body. As my lips clamped and swallowed, that energy seemed to burst between my thighs. Hod's thumb grazed over my clit, his cock filling me even more deeply, I tipped over the edge in turn, clutching Baldur's hip for balance.

My body clenched around Hod, and his movements turned jerky. He looped his arm around my waist, holding me to him as he spilled himself inside me. His mouth feathered kisses along my shoulder.

Baldur sank to the floor to kiss me on the mouth. I ended up tucked between the two of them, my head on Hod's shoulder and my hand on Baldur's thigh, as we lingered in the afterglow.

"Maybe you're right. A little darkness isn't a bad thing," Baldur murmured in a wry tone.

I laughed a little breathlessly. "No. Not at all." I squeezed his leg affectionately and snuggled closer to Hod's chest. In a minute or two, we'd have to break out of this joyful state and go back to reality, but I was going to enjoy this moment for as long as we could drag it out. "And three can definitely be more fun than two."

Hod snorted. "Suddenly I'm very glad there's only the four of us—unattached, anyway—in all of Asgard."

I swatted him. "I wouldn't want anyone else anyway. Four is more than enough, thank you very much."

His comment started my thoughts spinning in a totally different direction, though—to Freya, soaring home after her search for her daughter. To all those empty halls where Asgard's other inhabitants had once lived.

"The other gods who did used to live here," I said slowly. "Most of them are still around somewhere, right? They just took off to take an extended beach vacation or whatever?"

"As far as we know," Hod said. "Why, are you rethinking that 'four is more than enough' remark?"

I rolled my eyes. "No. I was just thinking that more gods would be helpful if we're supposed to be taking on a giant and his entire army. Shouldn't we go looking for the others? If Surt takes over the only stable realms left, it'll affect all of them too. This *is* still their original home."

Baldur shifted. "We could mention it to Odin."

Every nerve in my body balked. "No. Do you really think he'll say okay when he's shot down every other idea we've given him? He's too stuck on whatever he thinks is the right way for this to all go down."

"I won't argue with you there, valkyrie," Hod said. "But we do need him."

I tipped my head up to look at his face. "Do we really?"

That question hung in the air for the space of several heartbeats. A hint of a smile touched Hod's face. "All right," he said. "Supposing we don't... Shall we come up with a few plans of our own?"

16

Aria

The spray of the vast waterfall tickled over my face and bare arms. I swooped lower, but the only figures I could make out anywhere nearby were a couple of kids a little older than Petey who were splashing their feet in the lake at the base of the torrent.

Thor was shaking his head when I soared up to meet him at the edge of the rushing river. "I'm not sure where else to look," he said. "Njord ruled over the seas, so he has an affinity for water... If he's not hanging around any of his favorite spots, he could be anywhere along the coastlines or major lakes."

I motioned to the campsite we'd found, the stones around it marked with a few faded runes that Thor had said would have brought warmth overnight and repelled animal intrusions. "Do you have any idea how long it's been since he used that site?"

"The ashes from the firepit have been washed away by rain, and even the scorch marks on the rocks are worn down," Thor said. "I'd guess at least a few years."

I made a face. Thor and I had come down to Midgard to search out any of the gods who might be lingering there—Loki might have covered ground faster, but he'd pointed out that most of the gods wouldn't exactly welcome the sight of him. So far, the thunder god and I hadn't had much luck. This campsite was as close as we'd gotten to finding any of Asgard's former residents.

"At least we know he was still around that recently," I said, trying to look on the bright side. "You'd think they'd stop by their old home every now and then just to see how things are going."

"Ah, we didn't all part ways on the most favorable of terms," Thor said. "After our return from Ragnarok, a lot of things changed. Marriages broke apart, friendships turned sour. The war rubbed most of us caught up in it pretty raw."

"But not you?" I said with a lift of an eyebrow. I'd seen Thor conflicted now and then, but he'd never talked about that earlier war with the sort of horror I'd heard from the others.

He shrugged as he sent his lightning crackling over one of the stones with a message in case the sea god returned any time soon. *You're needed in Asgard.*

"I fought as well as I could," he said. "Our enemies were clear. I'd been in a lot more battles than any of the others except maybe Odin and Freya—and even they are just watching over the field as often as they're on it."

"You were in your element."

He chuckled. "Something like that. And also, my death was brief, since it happened right at the end. I can't begin to imagine how hard it was for those like Hod and Baldur who were left to linger in death so long."

Even though those words were serious, that comment brought back my interlude with the twins in Valhalla yesterday—the heat of Baldur's kisses, the caress of Hod's hands, the moments when it'd felt as if we existed only for each other.

"I think they're getting past that," I said.

Thor shot me a knowing grin. "A little help never hurts."

We set off over the landscape again, but our flight was more aimless now. I rubbed my arms as the wind buffeted my wings. "What do you think our chances are of just stumbling on any of them? Freya's been searching for her daughter for days with no luck."

"We're doing everything we can," Thor said. "At this point, we may have to rely on the messages we've left. I can't believe none of them ever return to their favorite haunts anymore."

"But they might not return before Surt decides to make his move." How long could we afford to wait before we took him on by ourselves? Not even Odin admitted to knowing how large his army might be already. Even if the giant would have preferred to wait another decade to grow it larger, he had to be aiming to start his invasion as soon as possible now that his plans had been exposed.

"Whatever happens, we'll put him down," Thor said, but he frowned after he'd spoken.

He thought of a couple more spots for us to check: a

mountainside hut from which Heimdall the gatekeeper had apparently liked to survey the realm of humankind and a stretch of apple farms where Idunn might have taken comfort. Neither turned up any godly presence. Thor etched his message here and there, his frown deepening.

"It's getting late," he said. "I think *we* should be returning to Asgard now."

My body protested at the thought of giving up our search, but obviously we couldn't count on the other gods being the solution to our problems. With a sigh, I swiveled toward the rainbow bridge.

We passed Heimdall's former hall, an ivory structure that clung to the side of the cliff next to the bridge. "He used to spend all day sitting on his front step, watching who'd come and go," Thor told me. "His eyes were as sharp as Loki's. The two of them never got along all that well. Maybe because he always spotted what the trickster might be up to sooner than the rest of us."

"At least Loki usually got you out of any trouble he got you into, right?" I said. And the gods had brought plenty of trouble down on Loki, too, not that any of them seemed to think of that most of the time.

"He did, he did. We'd have been much worse off without him. I believed that even before, in spite of everything. It was never as simple as hero or villain with him."

Those words lingered with me after we'd reached the city. "Should we scrounge up some dinner?" Thor suggested, but my mind was already leaping ahead of me.

"I'll grab some food later," I said. "There's something I want to check first."

Thor studied me. "Do you need company?"

"There are a few things I can do without godly assistance," I said, jabbing a finger at him with a smile to show I wasn't offended. He laughed and waved me off.

I didn't think he'd have seen me off that easily if he'd known exactly what I was planning on checking. I soared over to Valhalla and tucked my wings close to my back as I hurried down the length of the room. The one table was still askew where Baldur had leaned against it yesterday. I tugged my gaze away. I was interested in memories right now, but not my own.

The empty space around Yggdrasil closed against my skin as I stepped onto the bark-covered path. Sometimes the still blackness around it unnerved me. Today, there was something steadying about it. All the places I'd seen with Thor today, all those disappointments—they fell away as I walked with smooth strides along the trunk toward the branch that would lead me to Muspelheim. I paused at the base of that branch, breathing in slow and deep until my heart beat in an even rhythm. Then I pushed myself through the gate into the realm of fire.

Dodging the watchful dragon came instinctively now. I flattened myself under the sheltering ridge, waited until it had settled, and slipped away through the shadows. The heat of the realm penetrated even those dark patches, bringing sweat to my skin in a minute.

I hadn't come here to spy this time, though. I wanted to be found—just not by any monsters with jagged teeth and talons.

When I'd left the dragon far enough behind, I ventured out onto the dry plain at the foot of the cliff. I kept my wings spread, providing me with a little shade. The silver-white glimmer would stand out against the dark gray rock. I ambled along, waiting for the prickle of that being-watched sensation.

I'd just reached the edge of one of those rivers of magma when the feeling came over me. I stopped, a thicker heat wafting up from the churning liquid with its pulsing red glow. Maybe I didn't want to be standing quite this close to a substance that could mean my instant death for this conversation. I backed up a few steps and turned slowly.

My watcher was nowhere to be seen, but I'd expected that.

"Muninn," I called out, loud enough for my voice to carry but not so loud I thought it would disturb the distant dragon. "I came to talk to you. Peacefully." I held out my arms, my hands open. No weapons except the switchblade always in my pocket, and I didn't think the raven woman was all that scared of it.

The seconds slipped by with the trickle of a bead of sweat down my back. Had she said everything she'd wanted to last time? Maybe she didn't like the idea of giving in when someone else was trying to call the shots.

I was debating my next moves when a black flutter appeared at the edge of my vision. My head jerked around.

Muninn landed as she transformed, her pale limbs steadying her on the ground with her usual awkward grace. She'd left several feet between us, as if she didn't totally trust me not to lunge at her even with just my hands as weapons. If this had been right after we'd escaped from her prison, that would have been a reasonable fear.

She cocked her head. "What brings you here looking for me, valkyrie? I thought you had no interest in talking."

I swallowed, my throat rough from the dry heat. "You told me things before that you wanted me to keep in mind. You were right. I was hoping you might know other information that you'd be willing to share."

Her expression didn't change, her dark eyes sharp, her lips curved with mild curiosity. "What sort of information?"

"You used to travel all over the realms with Odin and on your own, didn't you?" I said. "I want to find the gods who've left Asgard. Maybe you've seen places where they liked to spend time that the others wouldn't know about. Or you got ideas about where they might go from their memories."

Muninn grimaced. "I have no interest in adding to Asgard's numbers. If the gods wish to return, they can find their own way back."

"We'll have more options for setting things right if we have more of them on our side," I said. "Isn't that what you want?"

She shifted her weight from one foot to the other. "I don't know what you mean."

I had to stop myself from gritting my teeth. "Why did you tell me about the dark elves? Don't you want us to fix what's wrong with the other realms? How are we supposed to do that when we know Surt could be storming Asgard any day now?"

"I suppose that's for you to figure out."

"That's all you're going to say?"

Her near-black eyes stared back at me unwaveringly. My hands clenched. "I want to fix things. None of us wants to see the realms failing—well, I don't know how Odin feels, but the rest of us will do whatever we can."

A rasp of a laugh escaped her. "If Odin will let you, hmm?"

"He's not *my* master," I said, and she flinched.

"He isn't mine anymore either," she said, her shoulders shifting as if she were about to slide back into raven form. "If you want answers, he knows more than I do."

"You know it's not that simple." I let out a sound of frustration and forced my voice to soften. "Please. Do you really want to see Midgard and Asgard burned down? You're angry with Odin—I get it. I don't like him all that much either. But he's just one god."

"The ruler of Asgard," Muninn spat out. "The one whose orders you'll all follow in the end."

"No," I said. "We won't. Not if we have other ways. Are you looking to bring the realms back to how they're meant to be, to stop whatever problems he caused, or is this just about getting revenge on him? Because if it's the latter, you're not really any better than him, are you?"

Muninn bristled. "*You're* like him," she said. "You push everyone else to do what you want, and where will that leave us in the end? With him still lording over all of us. He could *never* pay us back. Never. He'll never admit or believe he's done anything wrong. Deal with him, and then I'll deal with you."

She spun around and darted into the air with a rippling of black feathers. After a few flaps of her wings, she was nothing but a dark speck against the flat gray sky.

17

Loki

As hard as it sometimes was to believe, certain areas of the realm of giants were actually rather peaceful. The snowy mountains to the far north, for example, had been one of my favorite places to escape to long ago, before I'd come to Asgard, when the company of my supposed kin had grated on me too much. And this pine forest to the west, deeper into it than the realms inhabitants usually ventured—perhaps it was a relief to escape here from my godly oath-sworn kin too.

The breeze carried a crisp chill and the pines' sharp scent. Fallen needles crinkled under my feet as I wandered the lonely landscape. To tell the truth, I'd been hoping to find it a little less lonely. The gods of Asgard might have disdained the company of giants, but they'd been more than happy to take advantage of Jotunheim's more isolated corners when nowhere in Midgard appealed to them in their current mood. It had become increasingly difficult to find any part of the human realm that mortals hadn't penetrated.

I found no sign of any recent passage here, though. The only evidence I'd come across was proof that my former home was succumbing to the same decline that Hod had reported from Nidavellir. Many of the pines were stooping, their trunks weakened by some ailment I didn't recognize. The mountains, when I'd visited them earlier, had shaken once with an ominous tremor. I'd kept my distance from the towns and cities, but the dry earth and the constant chill despite it being summer made me wonder how well any crops were growing here.

It couldn't hurt to leave a few signs of my own, on the off-chance Bragi meandered this way in the following weeks to find inspiration for a poetic verse, or Skadi came seeking that wintry chill. They might not have been overjoyed if they'd seen me, but I didn't think they'd ignore an urgent call back to Asgard.

With a flick of my fingers, I inscribed a new message into the trunk of one of the wider pines. The tangy smoke tickled my nose. I turned to survey the forest, hesitating. I couldn't think of any other secret places the gods might have declined to tell their real kin they liked to travel to, but the thought of returning to Asgard empty-handed didn't sit well either.

No doubt Hod would have some snarky remark about where I might have gone. Or perhaps I'd find Thor had been searching for me again, wanting to make sure I hadn't gotten myself into any trouble. If only they'd spent a little more time focusing on the real source of so much of our troubles...

I pushed that thought aside and set off toward the gate that had brought me through to Jotunheim. I had a lot of ground to cover. And I couldn't say I enjoyed the thought of running into any of this realm's inhabitants.

The forest gave way to scruffy tundra at the edge of the giants' realm. Coarse tufts of grass sprouted here and there on the cracked earth, which was packed so hard my footsteps might have carried for miles if I'd let them touch the ground. Not that there was anyone around to hear my passage anyway. Or so I thought until a gravelly bellow called out to me.

"Sly One! I've been waiting for you."

I whirled around, propelling a burst of flame into my hand. There were few who'd be looking for me here who wouldn't be hoping for a fight, preferably one ending with my head on a pike.

The looming figure I found standing at the edge of the forest would have liked that, perhaps more than anyone.

Surt had always been a giant among giants. Even now, with the age that had finally started to catch up with him leaving his shoulders slightly hunched, he stood a few inches taller than my formidable height and nearly as broad as our Thunderer. His steel-gray hair hung lank above his glittering hazel eyes, his beard long and grizzled enough to rival Odin's.

He held himself in what should have been a casual stance, his arms loosely crossed and his weight leaned to one side. My gaze couldn't help catching on the broad sword he was gripping, though.

"Blazing One," I replied, encouraging the flames to rise from my palm with a twitch of my fingers. "Are you looking for a good scorching?"

Surt chuckled, a low rough sound. "Feel free to try me," he said. "My sword is always hungry for more."

Yes, it was that damned sword I had to be most wary of. A fiery gleam leapt along its length even now. Anything I threw at Surt, it could absorb and spew back at me, now or some later even more inopportune time. My chances of felling this giant alone were slim. But then, so were his of felling me. I could speed away from here in an instant on my shoes of flight.

"What do you want then?" I demanded. "Why would you wait for me *here* of all places?"

"I have underlings watching every gate at my disposal," Surt said. "One saw you emerge here from your realm. Your great tree won't let me through to speak to you in Asgard, and your companions didn't appear to take well to my attempt at a bridge. This seemed a better meeting spot."

"Well done," I said. "You've found me. I'm still waiting to hear the purpose of this 'meeting.'"

Surt's narrow eyes studied me for a long enough moment that my body tensed even further. "I think this meeting has been a long time coming," he said. "Don't you? Tell me, trickster, are you really all that satisfied with the choices you've made?"

"Perhaps you could be a little more specific," I suggested. "I'd estimate I make verging on a thousand choices every day. My breakfast this morning was quite satisfying, if that's what you're concerned about."

His expression didn't waver. He motioned to the landscape around us, his gaze still fixed on my face. "You left behind your home. Forsook your people for those shining ones of Asgard." His teeth gnashed on that last word, as if he could chew it up and spit it out. "And what have they ever given you? Chains and poison? What a poor puppet you are, slinking back to them after you'd brought them to their knees."

The "puppet" comment rankled. "It *was* my choice to remain there," I said. "Clearly you know nothing about my life. If all you came to do is rant about events from eons ago, I'll take my leave now."

I moved to turn on my heel.

"Loki," Surt said, straightening up. He stepped toward me, but his sword stayed down at his side. "You know we have more kinship than you share with any of those lordly beings up in their bright city. Have you forgotten where you began so quickly?"

"Oh, believe me, I remember quite well," I said. "In particular, I remember why I left it. Nothing I've seen since then has led me to regret that decision. I'll take the arrogant over the brutes, thank you."

"The brutes." Surt shook his head. "Come? I will show you something."

"And why should I want to see anything *you* would want to show me?"

His eyes glittered. "Because of all the beings in Asgard, you at least care to know everything you possibly can. Or have they finally taught you how to close your mind like they do theirs?"

He strode off along the line of trees, his sword swinging at his side. I grimaced at myself and followed after him, keeping a safe distance. Our greatest enemy stood before me. It would be foolhardy to ignore anything he might be willing to share. I gathered knowledge, yes— so I could use it to my advantage when I needed to. If wielded properly, a fact could be a sharper weapon than any blade.

Surt's powerful legs carried him swiftly even if he couldn't leave the ground. I had to walk briskly to keep up. We passed the span of forest where I'd done my searching and veered across the mostly barren ground toward what appeared to be a narrow valley carved into the hard-packed earth.

The giant stopped at the edge of the wide crevice. He swept his free hand toward it.

"This is what's become of our homeland. The ground itself will not hold. It splits and breaks as if wrenching itself apart."

I tipped my head to one side. "A bit of a hassle for one passing through, I suppose, but hardly a catastrophe."

Surt whirled toward me, a surge of fire hissing along his blade. "Do you think this is the only one? The only place? The earth opened beneath the capital a few years ago. It swallowed hundreds with their houses. And there were more before and since."

"Ah," I said, keeping my expression and my voice blank. I hadn't actually discovered that yet. I hadn't had all that much time for venturing around Jotunheim since our escape from Muninn's prison, and I'd had no access for decades before then. This was worse than I would have imagined.

Odin had known, hadn't he? How could he have failed to notice a crumpled city in his constant peering from his high seat?

"And do you intend to seal the earth back together through some magic you haven't shared with me yet?" I inquired. "How does your great plan to rip apart the realms that remain untouched help anyone, really, in the long run?"

"Do you know why the realms are falling apart?" Surt asked. "Why only Asgard and Midgard hold steady? Surely the great mind of Loki can put the pieces together."

Asgard was the realm of the gods, and Midgard lay at the center of it all. That was how we'd explained it when we'd discussed it between ourselves. But it wasn't really an answer, was it? What was so special about Midgard, really, other than it being a land far more appealing to myself and my companions than any other...

Or perhaps that was my answer right there.

"The gods used to visit all of the realms regularly," I said slowly. "Now we rarely venture beyond those two."

"And still you say 'we' as if they'll ever truly let you be one of them." Surt made a scoffing sound. "This is all their doing. My imprisonment in Muspelheim. The fracturing of the realms. They can't be bothered to act as the caretakers they take such pride in being. And you'd stand by them still?"

"As opposed to standing with you while you burn everything else to the ground?" I retorted.

"Oh, there *will* be burning," Surt said. "But only as long as it takes to claim the better lands we're owed. There's plenty of room in Asgard and Midgard to fit us, isn't there? The humans will adjust to a little extra servitude. Perhaps they'll be better off. And this time it'll be the gods who are chained. We'll bring them down to the realms, force them to lend their powers to healing these worlds, as they rightfully should."

He sliced his sword through the air, and the fire in it warbled. "I can do it faster and more cleanly with you alongside me, Loki. You're worthy of greater honors than they'll ever offer you. Stand with me and take what should be yours, and we'll divide the realms between us. Isn't it time they lost the upper hand? You can save the realms they always claimed you would destroy."

His words tugged at something deep inside me. The bitter anger in them stirred a matching emotion I'd so often buried. Suddenly I understood him so well I could have cringed and laughed at the same time. My fingers curled into my palms. Oh, I knew that anger, all right.

I'd seen Surt's brutality with my own eyes, all those centuries ago—but then, I'd also seen plenty of brutality from the gods. After all this time under their heels, kicked about like a dog they didn't want at the dinner table... The thought of taking the reins and putting them in their places did have a certain appeal. I could be a kinder jailer than they'd ever been to me.

A sickly satisfaction spread through me at the idea. How many times had I dreamed of a moment like this, all those ages ago? I could be brutal too, in my own ways, when the situation called for it. Could I really say I got no enjoyment from it at all?

Perhaps Surt was right. We were more alike than I'd wanted to consider.

I studied the giant, and resolve solidified in my chest. There *was* something to be gained here after all.

"I may entertain your offer," I said. "Perhaps we should discuss it further in your own kingdom, behind walls where Odin has no chance of overhearing?"

Surt grinned. "Come along then, and we'll see where we end up."

18

Aria

Evening had fallen as I sprawled on my stomach at the edge of the grassy cliff-edge where Asgard fell away into the sky. The rainbow bridge's surface still shimmered. When Loki came loping across its arc, glints of its color caught in his pale red hair and cast his paler skin in odd shades.

His gaze was distant, his expression unusually serious. I sat up, and it was only then that he seemed to notice I was there.

"Pixie," he said, coming to a stop at the foot of the bridge. "Playing watchdog?"

I wasn't completely sure what he meant, but it did probably look a little odd for me to be perched here.

"I was thinking about Heimdall watching the bridge all the time when he still lived here," I said. "Trying to figure out where someone like that would want to go if he *wasn't* here. So far it hasn't really helped, though."

I expected Loki to stroll over and join me, or else to beckon me to join him, but he just stood there, his stance a little stiff. A tickle of uneasiness ran down my back.

"We gave the search our best shot," he said. "At this point I assume if the other gods care to join us, they'll have to do it by their own steam."

I pushed myself to my feet. Loki didn't exactly pull away from me as I walked over to him, but he did start striding on toward the city as if it didn't matter to him all that much whether I reached him. The tickling niggled deeper.

"Hey," I said, jogging the last few steps to grab his elbow. "What's the hurry? Did something happen down there?"

He stopped and arched an eyebrow as he peered down at me. "Nothing of note. I'm merely tired of rushing to and fro searching for those who apparently care so little what happens to this place. There's leftover roast in my cold room I had a mind to eat, and a bed I'm looking forward to collapsing onto."

He was talking in his usual wry tone, but there was something distant about it too. I inhaled as I decided what to say next, and a whiff of a smoky chemical smell seeped into my nose, just barely perceptible to my heightened valkyrie senses. I leaned closer, and Loki eased away from me.

It had come from him. I knew that smell. It was the stink of Muspelheim.

Why would he have risked going there alone? And if

he'd gone there, how could he have been coming back over the rainbow bridge? I'd been sitting by it since Thor and I had gotten back—I'd have known if Odin had directed it somewhere other than Midgard.

If Loki had been acting like normal, I'd have asked him directly, but the distance in his demeanor made me balk.

"Where did you search?" I asked, keeping my tone as casual as I could manage. "It seemed like Thor and I covered most of Midgard. But maybe you know different places than he does."

"Oh, here and there." The trickster waved his hand dismissively. "There's a lot of world to cover in that realm of yours." He gave me a smile that would have settled my nerves if I hadn't known he'd just lied to me.

My stomach twisted. I didn't know how to confront him on that lie. Loki could talk his way out of just about anything. If he didn't want to admit what he'd been up to, there was no chance in hell I'd pry the truth out of him.

"Okay," I said. "Well, go enjoy that roast of yours."

He tipped his head to me. For a second I thought he might lean in for a kiss. But he pulled himself back and hurried on toward his hall, leaving me with an ache that stretched from my gut to my heart.

Loki had been more tense than I remembered from our first few weeks together ever since we'd escaped from Muninn's prison, but that made sense. He'd been faced with horrors as traumatic as anything I'd been through, ones I was sure he'd buried to keep the peace with the other gods. And he'd obviously been frustrated that they weren't willing to force the issue of Odin's past actions with the Allfather yet.

This was something different, though. He'd never been so standoffish with *me*. I was his valkyrie, the one he'd chosen. If he didn't even think he could trust me with the truth of what he'd been doing...

I didn't know how to follow that thread to a logical conclusion. Or maybe I did, but none of the conclusions I could draw sat right with me. Biting my lip, I wandered into the city along the same path he'd taken.

Loki had already disappeared into his hall—assuming that was where he'd really been going. I paused partway down the road, unsure of where *I* wanted to go.

The door to Thor's huge hall eased open, and the thunder god came out onto the threshold.

"Is everything all right?" he asked. "You look a bit lost."

"I'm okay," I said. "I just..." I rubbed my face. I didn't know what to say about it either.

"Do you want to come in?"

Thor's tone was soft, but a thread of heat wove through it anyway. I paused, tugged by a totally different sort of emotion. I never had made good on the promise that he'd only have to wait a few more hours to enjoy each other's company after we'd been interrupted the other morning.

And I didn't really want to be alone right now, with this uneasiness creeping through me.

"I think I would," I said, and went to meet him in the doorway.

I hadn't paid a whole lot of attention to his hall when

I'd snuck in here that night, other than to figure out where the bedroom was. In the clearer light of the evening, I was struck by just how vast the place really was. The ceiling loomed far enough over the central hall to have held two floors instead of just the one, and at least a couple dozen doors lined that hall.

"This is an awful lot of space for one guy," I said. "Even a guy as big as you." I knuckled Thor's arm affectionately.

He chuckled. "Well, it wasn't always only mine."

Oh, right. "You were married," I said. "Before."

"Before Ragnarok. Yes. Sif." He said her name easily and evenly, so I guessed that split hadn't been too painful. Or maybe it'd just happened so long ago that he'd had more than enough time to get over it. Curiosity pricked at me anyway.

"What happened?" I asked. "You said before that a lot of people went their separate ways afterward, everyone was so shook up. Was it just that?"

"That was some of it. She was definitely shaken." He rested his hand on my shoulder blade and ushered me down the hall. "She didn't want me to leave on any more adventuring, and she couldn't stand that Loki and I made peace with each other. She and him..." He paused, the corner of his mouth quirking up. "I was furious at the time. She had the most gorgeous hair, even closer to gold than Freya's is, and one day he got it into his head to chop it all off when she was sleeping. He never did own up to why. Maybe it was part of that ruckus-raising Odin ordered him to do."

A shadow crossed the thunder god's face then. I

slipped my hand around his and squeezed. "What happened?"

"Oh, I yelled at him some, and he promised me he'd only been making way for an even finer head of hair for her. Off he flew down to Nidavellir to have the dark elves craft some—out of actual gold. It really was the most lovely thing. *She* liked it, even though she didn't want to admit it. And I got Mjolnir out of that same bargain. As far as I'm concerned, all's well that ends well. Sif... Sif could hold quite a grudge."

He'd patted the hammer hanging from his belt when he mentioned it. My stomach knotted all over again. The story he was telling me—it was another side of the story that had ended with Loki's mouth sewn shut because the gods had judged against him on his bet.

That memory still stung Loki. Thor smiled when he talked about it. He hadn't been there in the memory Muninn had constructed, so who knew how much he knew about that incident, but he had to be aware of the consequences the trickster god had faced.

Maybe it wasn't surprising that Loki sometimes retreated into himself, even from me. He'd had to hold so much in for so long. Keeping up that slyly cheerful front must have gotten exhausting.

That still didn't explain him outright lying about sneaking off to Muspelheim, though.

Thor motioned me into a side room where a cushioned bench squatted next to a low table. The table was laid with bread, various fruits, and a hunk of cheese.

"Already time for your second dinner?" I teased.

"Who says I ever finished my first one?" Thor replied with a grin.

The niggling doubts stayed with me as I sat on the bench next to him. I picked up a strawberry and bit into it, but the tart juice on my tongue wasn't enough to distract me.

"Loki hasn't gotten into any 'trouble' since then— since Ragnarok—has he?" I said. "It seems like all the stories I've heard are from before."

"Nothing extreme enough that I remember it," Thor said. "And from what I remember, he was very contrite when we first returned. He has his sly ways about him, for his own amusement, and he certainly enjoys prodding those he doesn't get along with on occasion, but... Well, even before, he was rarely actually cruel."

"There was no reason for him to be stirring up chaos anymore," I said.

"No. I suppose not." Thor shook his head. "If he'd been allowed to be completely on our side, I can't help wondering if we could have avoided Ragnarok altogether."

I blinked at him. "Odin seems to think it had to happen." None of the other gods, even Loki, had indicated they didn't agree with that one thing.

"And maybe he's right," the thunder god said. "He would know better than me. But with Loki's cleverness... I suppose Odin is the only person he could never quite outwit. If he'd put that mind to use fighting for us, I can only imagine how differently that final battle might have gone."

He looked at the cheese sandwich he'd been putting

together as if he couldn't remember why he'd thought he was hungry. His forehead furrowed. "I suppose it's silly for me to think *I* could come up with some sort of scheme."

"Of course not," I said. "Just because he's clever doesn't mean he's got all the wits in Asgard. Why? Did you have a scheme?"

Thor waved me off. "It's nothing. The others made that clear."

"No, come on." I scooted closer to him, setting my hand on his arm. "*I* want to hear about it."

He was silent for a long moment. Then he set down the sandwich and ran his fingers through his thick hair. His gaze slid away from me as if he were afraid to watch my reaction while he spoke. There was something sweet about how nervous he was to share this part of himself.

"I've thought, the way the giants are—Surt's been apart from them for so long, and they always did squabble amongst themselves as it was—they're so easily tricked if they think something they want is in reach, or that they have to avenge themselves of some slight... Perhaps we could find a way to use them against Surt. Make them our army without them even realizing who they're fighting for." He ducked his head. "Just a vague idea."

"It sounds like a good idea to me," I said, imagining a horde of giants charging toward Surt's fortress. "Why don't you tell the others and figure out the rest with them?"

Thor made a pained expression. "I tried. They brushed me off and went on with their own planning. It's not as if I've been a fountain of wisdom in the past, you know. I'm the Thunderer."

"Hey." I poked him in the arm so he'd look at me. "That doesn't mean they shouldn't pay attention when you do have an idea. And anyway, you're not just thunder, are you? You've got lightning. Why focus only on the loud and strong side when you can be quick and sharp too?"

His mouth opened and closed again before he managed to answer. "That's a very good question," he said. "I've spent so much time thundering around, it's easy to forget how powerful even one bolt of electricity can be."

Even a small one. "I haven't forgotten," I said, thinking of the sparks that had danced from his fingertips over my body during that interlude in Muninn's prison. A sudden heat pooled low in my belly, urged on by the warmth of his body right next to mine. I lowered my eyelashes, trying out a little slyness myself. "I'm always happy to offer myself up as a test subject if you need a little practice to jog your memory."

Thor looked at me so intently that the temperature in the room seemed to rise by a few degrees. "Is that so?" he said, his already low voice even huskier than before.

I touched the side of his face, and he bent down to kiss me. His hot breath mingled with mine, with a twitch of his tongue against my lips that sent an electric tingle through me. Oh, yes, that'd been a good talk, but I was ready for more now.

I murmured encouragingly, gripping the front of his shirt. Thor kissed me again and again with more hunger each time. His hands started to trail up and down my sides. Each brush of his fingertips, even through the thin fabric of my tank top, sent a fresh burst of quivers over my skin.

When he slid his palm around to cup my breast, I pressed into his touch, kissing him harder. His thumb swiveled over the swell of flesh, and a spark danced over the tip. I whimpered as my nipple hardened in an instant.

He teased it for a minute longer through my top before moving his sizzling torture to the other side. Then he eased his hand under my shirt to caress me without interference. His fingers stroked and flicked, each point of pressure like a tiny jolt of lightning. I yanked him closer to me, moaning.

His hand dipped lower, to my jeans. A tremble of need ran through me as he tugged open my fly. He slid his fingers right inside my panties, his breath catching when he felt the dampness already gathered there. A zap of pleasure jolted over my clit, and my hips jerked. I gasped.

"Oh, God." Just like that, I was already so close to release. I groped down his body to pay him back in kind, but Thor eased back and caught my wrist. His other hand stayed between my thighs, his thumb slicking from my clit to my folds and back again.

"I want to watch you," he said thickly. His brown eyes smoldered with longing. "I want to see just how good I can make you feel, no distractions."

I swallowed hard, my chest tightening with emotion. So much emotion, swelling inside me, that I didn't know what to do with.

I'd said I loved Hod's darkness. What could I say about Thor? I loved his strength. I loved his compassion— and his passion too. I could have said that, but it didn't feel like enough to encompass even half of the feelings surging through me.

Thor's fingers twitched with another electric tingle, and every other feeling was overwhelmed but the pleasure racing through me. I tipped my head back, bucking to meet his hand, giving myself over to everything he wanted to give me.

19

Aria

I might have slept a little longer that morning if an enormous but joyful bellow hadn't shaken the floor beneath my bed.

"Tyr!"

If Thor was that happy, whatever was going on couldn't be a bad thing. I sat up, rubbing my eyes, and went to see what the fuss was about.

Asgard's other current inhabitants were also gathering in the courtyard the shout had rung out from. At first I couldn't see anything except Thor's broad form. Then he stepped back from his embrace to reveal a lanky man with bronze-brown hair that fell to his shoulders. The new arrival looked older than my gods and younger than Odin, maybe late thirties or early forties if I could have judged by human standards, the corners of his eyes slightly crinkled. His face held the same divine attractiveness as every god I'd met so far.

He was also missing a hand. The base of his right arm, just before where his wrist should have been, ended in a smooth stump, the edges only faintly rippled with scar tissue.

"Quite the welcoming party," he said in a warm bass voice. "Maybe I should have come back sooner."

"It's good to see you," Baldur said. "Where have you been?"

"Oh, mostly rambling around southern and eastern Europe," Tyr said. "All sorts of interesting developments in those areas recently."

"Tyr's domains are law and combat," Thor said, catching my eye. "And it's been at least a couple centuries since we last saw him." He clapped the other god on the back.

Another war god? I guessed between this guy, Odin, and Freya, they covered all the possible angles.

"Although interestingly, neither domain explains how he lost his hand," Loki said, his tone managing to sound both light and caustic at the same time. "It's such a shame it wasn't reborn with the rest of you, isn't it?"

Tyr gave the trickster a wary glance and seemed to decide to ignore him. "I gathered Asgard was in need," he said, turning back to Thor. "Although the message I came across was rather vague."

"Hmm," Odin said. I flinched—I hadn't heard the king of the gods approaching behind me. "There is a certain strength in numbers. Welcome home."

"Come," Thor said. "We'll explain everything we

know so far. The most important part is that Surt has reappeared, and he means to make good on every threat he made in the past and more."

He motioned Tyr toward his hall. Baldur, Hod, and Freya moved to join them. Loki wavered, his jaw tight. Before I could decide whether to follow the others or go to him and find out what was bothering him, Odin's hand closed over my shoulder.

"Valkyrie," he said, the word holding no admiration when *he* said it. "I think we need to have a talk of our own."

Loki's gaze darted our way. "What business could you have with her?" he said, his eyes much darker than the mild curiosity in his voice warranted.

"Oh, it seems we have a great deal to discuss," Odin said. He tipped his head in the direction the other gods had gone. "Don't let that keep you from staying abreast of the plans being made."

They stared each other down for a moment, king and trickster, the tension prickling over my skin. Loki lifted one narrow shoulder in a careless shrug. "I'll see if there's anything I can add to Tyr's education," he said, and strode off. My stomach tightened as he passed out of view, leaving Odin and me alone.

Odin nudged me in the opposite direction toward his hall, and I went, my heart thumping uneasily. "What's this about?" I said.

"All in good time," the Allfather said in a tone that didn't offer any room for argument.

My back itched, my wings eager to break free and carry me away from Odin and his foreboding presence. It was hard to think this conversation was going to be an enjoyable one, even if I didn't have any idea what he wanted to talk about. But running away hadn't been a very successful strategy when it came to the gods. It wasn't as if I could avoid ever coming back.

Maybe he just wanted to check in and see how I was doing after looking in on Petey the other day. A little regal concern toward his subjects. Ha ha ha.

When we reached his hall, Odin stepped into the fore-room where the group of us had always met him before. I hesitated in the middle of the thick soft rug as he settled into his throne-like chair. There was nowhere for me to sit in here unless I wanted to grab one of the pillows along the wall. I was pretty sure he expected me to stay standing while he peered down at me like he was doing right now. My hackles rose at his grim expression before he even started to speak.

"I've gathered that you've been diverting my gods from the course of action we decided on," he said. "As the sudden appearance of Tyr lends proof to."

"*Your* gods?" I repeated. "I'm pretty sure they belong to themselves. We're the ones who've been doing all the fighting while you've sat around back here making your plans."

"My plans that will ensure both our realm and your former one remain safe. Unless you've decided you no longer care about that cause."

I crossed my arms over my chest. "How exactly does finding more gods to join the fight hurt the cause?" Or finding out what was driving the dark elves, although if Odin didn't already know Hod had ventured into their realm, I wasn't going to spill the beans. "And why are you talking to *me* about this? We're all working together. I don't exactly call the shots."

He gave me a baleful look. "Do you truly believe it could have escaped me how much influence you've managed to gain over them? You've earned their loyalty through honest means, from what I've gathered. Let us not switch to dishonesty now."

How much had he seen, with all the spying he did from his high seat? I couldn't tell whether this was a bluff or he knew for sure I'd been the one to suggest we go searching for the other gods. He couldn't see through walls. How much had we discussed it outside?

"I'm not lying about anything," I said, which was technically true. Omissions didn't count, right? "I *honestly* believe that having more manpower makes it easier to win a war. I'd have thought that was common sense."

"This isn't a common war," Odin said, his voice rising to a rumble as he leaned forward in his chair. He glowered down at me for a moment, a fierce light in his brown eye, enough power emanating from his body that it took all my willpower not to cower. My arms went rigid at my sides.

"Fine," I said. "Nothing about this situation is normal to me. You want me to stop coming up with new plans? Tell me what the hell yours really *is*. Because you can't think that the six of us charging at Surt's fortress alone is going to win that war."

Odin leaned back in his chair slowly. He turned his

head toward the window across from us, his gaze going distant.

"I see things, you know," he said. "Not just from my high seat. Not just with my eye." He tapped the scarred patch above his other cheek. "I gave this one up for knowledge beyond what we can grasp in front of us. It comes to me in whispers and fragments... but it comes."

A shiver ran down my back. "And you've seen something about the battle with Surt?"

His gaze returned to me. "I know this much: No matter how many reinforcements you summon, our victory comes down to you five and the power you hold between you. That is what we must depend on. That is where we must build our strength. The rest may not matter at all."

You five and the power you hold. The chill that had touched me a second ago tickled deeper. "What exactly did you 'see'?" I asked. "What are we going to do?"

Nothing shifted in his eyes, which were flatly dull now. "I know only the wisdom that reaches me. That is what I must use to guide me. But if the answer is the five of you, then the five of you must focus on your strengths. Build on your power. This running around across the realms only weakens us."

"So, that really is your whole plan?" I said. "We charge in there at Surt and hope that we manage to destroy him and his army?"

"How much you're able to destroy will be up to you," Odin said. "When you're ready, I hope it will be enough to cripple him. Perhaps you will have to give your all to see the battle through, but that would be a worthy sacrifice."

"Give our all?" I stared at him. "You mean you think we're going to go down in the fight. I guess it'd be hard not to, if it all comes down to the five of us trying to wreck everything we can reach. And you really think because of some 'whispers and fragments' that's the best way to go? You're fine sending your sons and your blood-brother off to be slaughtered?" I didn't expect him to care at all about me, but the others... My jaw clenched. They deserved better than this.

"Perhaps any that fall will be reborn again as they were before," Odin said evenly.

"And maybe they won't. You admitted yourself you don't know if that's a guarantee."

"It is a chance they'll willingly take to save our realm." His eyes narrowed. "Will you?"

How could I answer that? If I could die knowing Petey would be safe for the rest of his life, the rest of the realms would be a bonus. But I couldn't believe that was the only way, not when there was so much Odin was refusing to consider or even admit to.

I could feel, standing there before him, that he wasn't going to budge, not this morning. Possibly not ever. I raised my chin.

"I'll fight for Asgard, and I'll fight for Midgard, wherever that takes me, whatever the risks," I said, meaning it. I kept the rest of my thoughts to myself. I'd also keep looking for other ways to fight, no matter what Odin thought about that. If he wanted to stop us, let him go ahead and try. So far he'd been a lot of talk and not a whole lot of action.

"Good," Odin said. "Then you know where to aim your focus. Make me glad to have a valkyrie in Asgard again, Aria."

"I'll do my best," I said, and the weird part was, I meant that too. Just not in the way he'd have wanted.

I fled Odin's hall as quickly as I could manage without totally embarrassing myself. The other gods were standing far down the road outside Thor's hall in a cluster of conversation. I guessed they hadn't made it all the way inside before Tyr had insisted on getting some answers.

No head of pale-flame hair stood out among them, though. I frowned, scanning the buildings around us, but Loki appeared to have vanished. Remembering how he'd spoken to Tyr and then Odin, the queasy feeling I'd had since he lied to me yesterday bubbled up again.

The trickster god was one of the five of us. Odin couldn't get mad at me for going looking for him, right?

I slipped away into the forest behind Odin's hall where Loki had found me the other day. No sign of him there, or in the orchard beyond it. I paused, listening, wishing that the bond between us that allowed him to track me worked both ways. If he'd been close, I could have sensed his presence like I'd found each of the gods in Muninn's prison, but he wasn't anywhere near here.

It'd be easier to track him down from above. I unfurled my wings and pushed off the ground. The air rushed over me as I swept myself higher and higher, until it seemed almost all of Asgard sprawled out beneath me. I soared over it, searching for a speck of red against the green landscape.

My gaze slid to the blue-gray line of the sea in the distance, almost the same stormy color as Petey's eyes. As I turned toward it, the faintest hint of salt met my tongue on the breeze. Like on the beach Loki had taken me to when he'd talked about his slaughtered children.

I flew toward the rocky span of shoreline. I didn't know how many miles I'd crossed before I made out a tall pale form standing there.

The flaps of my wings slowed. I glided closer, holding my breath. Would Loki want to be interrupted? I was thinking probably not, given that he'd gone this far to get away from the rest of us. What was he even doing out here?

Not much, from the looks of things. He was standing next to a large boulder. No, not standing—leaning against it with his forearms braced against it and his head bowed.

There was something so anguished in his posture that I hesitated, hovering, torn between going to him and giving him the solitude he'd obviously been looking for.

What was that rock? Why *here*? I hugged myself, the certainty I'd felt when I'd faced down Odin faltering.

I could stand up to the Allfather. I could encourage *my* gods to make other plans, try other strategies. But watching Loki slumped against that rock right now, it couldn't have been more clear that our problems ran deeper than that. And I didn't have a clue how to solve this one.

20

Thor

The costume I'd assembled wasn't half as ridiculous as the one I'd once worn to trick the giants. But then, it would have been hard to top a wedding dress. I was lucky Freya had ever forgiven me for that coarse impersonation.

Today I wasn't attempting to look like anyone in particular. I just needed to *not* look like myself.

"What do you think?" I asked Baldur. He was the only one of my companions I'd mentioned my intentions too. It would be a lot more satisfying to return victorious and show them the results than to listen to their doubts ahead of time—if I even got a word in edgewise—and a lot less embarrassing if nothing came of this gamble.

My younger brother looked me over with his head tipped to one side. "You can't do much to hide your size," he said. "But bulk isn't that unusual in giants anyway. I'm not sure *I'd* recognize you without your usual ten-day shadow if I hadn't been here to watch you shave it off."

I mock-glowered at him. "Be glad it'll grow back. Does the glamour look natural enough?"

He nodded. "It just lightens your usual color, in your hair and your face, not adding anything. And it should hold until you return."

He'd used his powers to wash out my appearance. My normally dark reddish-brown hair was now so pale it looked almost blond; my ruddy skin had turned peachy. Between that, going clean-shaven, and the fact that I hadn't adventured in Jotunheim in quite a while, I didn't think anyone would peg me for the Thunderer unless I gave myself away.

"You're leaving the hammer, I assume," Baldur added.

My hand dropped to Mjolnir where it hung from my belt. The thought of walking into giant territory without my greatest weapon, not even knowing I was going to retrieve it there, made my skin tighten. But that hammer would be more of a tip-off to my true identity than anything else.

I detached it and set it by Valhalla's wall. Amid the swords and spears mounted there, I spotted an axe. "This will do. A suitably giant-ish weapon."

I smiled as I removed it. Its handle was thick enough to fit on my belt exactly where I usually hung Mjolnir. I brushed my hands over the plain tunic and pants I'd chosen, dragging in a breath. "I suppose I'm ready to go, then."

"Are you sure it's wise for you to go alone?" Baldur

asked. "I could join you—as Father said, there's strength in numbers."

I shook my head. "I couldn't ask you—or any of the others. You're full-blooded Aesir. I at least have the giant heritage in my blood." Loki could pass, of course, and could shift himself into an even better disguise than I could ever manage, but this once, I wanted to make my way without the trickster smoothing the way. Let him see that I had some brains to go with my brawn.

"Good luck, then," Baldur said, squeezing my arm. "If you haven't returned by tomorrow, I'll have to sound the alarm."

"If I can't manage to do this by the end of the day, I deserve the shame of being subjected to a rescue," I said. "Don't worry yourself too much. How many times have I ventured into the realm of giants and returned as well as when I'd left?"

My brother smiled. "More than I can count."

Neither of us mentioned the fact that I'd never ventured there both without my hammer and completely alone.

"Should I be worrying about you?" I asked him as he accompanied me through the vast room to the hearth's entrance. "The darkness inside that you were struggling with—"

Baldur cut off my question with a gentle wave of his hand. "It seems I was fighting so hard against it I only made the pressure of it worse," he said. "I've started letting a little of it out here and there under my control, and I feel steadier every time I do. Nothing could quash my light."

"I never doubted that." I patted him on the back before stepping away from him to duck into the blackness of the hearth.

Yggdrasil's branch into Jotunheim brought me out nowhere all that near any of the major cities. It was the capital I was aiming for, where my ploy was most likely to reach the ears it needed to. Thankfully the isolated terrain where I emerged meant I could coast along with bursts of lightning-twined cloud until I reached one of the better-trafficked roads leading toward the realm's largest city.

A couple carting smoked meat in that direction gave me an uncertain look but agreed to let me ride in the back, as long as I helped them unload once they reached their shop in town. The only difficult part of the journey was restraining myself from sampling their merchandise, which I had to admit set my mouth watering. I could criticize giants for many things, but they did know how to eat well when they took a mind to do it right.

Perhaps that was where my great appetite came from. The thought settled uneasily in my gut, but I grasped onto it, setting my jaw. I was here as a giant. I had to embrace every bit of me that my mother's line might have affected.

Who would have thought it might be my giant side and not my godly nature that would help me save Asgard?

Unloading the cart only took a few minutes, even though I played down my strength so I didn't draw outright stares. Then it was a simple matter of spotting the most popular drinking establishment in town—the one where figures of some influence among their giant peers would be inclined to enjoy themselves.

The streets were quieter than I remembered being usual, but then, I'd only entered this city a few times in the past, and those times many centuries ago. I assumed it was just a slower night until I turned a corner and found myself faced with a chasm that ran straight through the road. It gaped several feet wide, and the buildings on either side had crumbled into it, leaving only ruins that no one had yet attempted to reconstruct. A makeshift bridge of wooden boards weighted with stones spanned it near the spot where I stood.

What calamity had caused this? I approached the chasm cautiously and peered down into its depths, finding only darkness where the sides narrowed. The couple with the cart had made some mutterings about the "splittings of the earth," but I'd assumed they were talking about a minor earthquake or the like near their farm.

Was this happening a lot? My memory slipped back to Hod's comments about the cave-ins in Nidavellir. Could the realm of giants be cracking open just as the dark elves' home was collapsing?

I wasn't sure I quite felt *sorry* for the giants, given our history, but the possibility left my nerves creeping with even more uneasiness. At least the general sense that their home was under threat should help me convince whoever listened to the story I had to tell.

I backtracked, not entirely trusting the rudimentary bridge under my substantial weight, and wandered farther through the streets. It wasn't long before a whiff of ale reached my nose. I followed it to a street lined with restaurants, shops, and taverns.

One particular tavern took up the space of two buildings on the edge of a cobblestone square, its windows bright and energetic voices already carrying through the open windows even though it was only mid-afternoon. That looked like a promising spot.

Girding myself, I pushed past the door into the dim light of the establishment. Giants sat around the many circular tables of heavy oak, most of them with tankards in hand. The barkeep behind the matching counter at the back of the place was just setting out several more frothing mugs for the patrons.

Several gazes turned my way at my entrance. This was where I had to find whatever cunning I had in me. I let my shoulders slump and lumbered over to the counter as if I had the weight of all nine realms resting on them.

"A glass of your best ale," I said, leaning against the counter. "Ah, no, make it two glasses. No doubt I'll need more than that before I'm through."

"Had a rough time of it?" the barkeep asked as he poured my drink.

"You could say that," I said. "But not as rough a time as we'll all have if something isn't done. Those bastards in Asgard! They've never missed the chance to lord it over us."

One of the giants sitting near me glanced over. "What's this about Asgard?" he asked, his face already flushing.

If there was one thing I knew about giants, it was that you didn't mention the highest realm unless you wanted to provoke some tempers.

I shook my head as if defeated. "There's no point in talking about it. Look at us. Look at this city. He's right. We're doomed."

A couple of the other giants nearby peered over at me. "What do you mean, doomed?" the first one demanded. "Speak plainly, will you? I'm not interested in guessing games."

I eyed him and the others looking our way, pretending to consider. My heart was thumping faster than if I'd been in the middle of a battle, or at least more anxiously.

I could do this. I could be sly—maybe not as well as Loki, but I'd watched him in action often enough, hadn't I?

Imagining the impressed shock on the trickster's face when he found out what I'd pulled off bolstered my confidence.

"Maybe you'll listen," I said. "The others I talked to were too slow to wrap their heads around it. But you— you seem to know what's what."

The giant drew himself up straighter. Another thing about giants: They were so easily manipulated by flattery. Especially when it came to the intelligence they were often accused, with good reason, of lacking. "I'll listen," he said.

Some of the others tugged their chairs closer. "What's going on?" a woman among them asked.

"I saw Surt today," I said. "I *spoke* to him."

A murmur passed through my audience. Even more heads turned my way. "Surt?" someone said. "I haven't heard talk of him in years. Wasn't he banished to Muspelheim for that failure of a war against the gods?"

Someone else snorted. "Some victory he brought us. Wipe them all out just for them to spring up again good as new."

"He was banished," I said, nodding. "But somehow he's sneaking back to our realm now and then. Maybe the gods are letting him. I have to think—the things he was saying—Odin must have done more than banish him. He must have Surt in his thrall."

"What are you talking about?" the first giant said.

I looked down at my hands as if it pained me to say this part. "He was ranting about how weak the jotun have become. How none of us deserve this realm. That the draugr he's been raising are better warriors than us. I think he means to take the realm by force. Why would he do that if the gods weren't behind him, urging him on through their awful powers?"

The murmur that rippled around me at that question sounded like agreement. I restrained the urge to smile. My ploy had worked. I'd hooked them.

"A draug fight better than a giant," the woman who'd spoken earlier muttered. "Any of us could take on ten."

"I tried to tell him that," I said. "But he just laughed. He said he's been building his army just to prove it to us. It was horrible, seeing him like that. I tried to tell the others I spoke to—we have to help him. Break him out of their spell. Or at least we have to *stop* him before he tears this realm apart even more than it's already been shaken."

"The latter would be simpler," the first giant said, with an uneven grin that told me I wouldn't need any more persuasion to send him on the path I wanted. "Surt thinks so highly of himself? I think he's lived far too long."

21

Aria

"Well," Tyr said, clapping his hands where he was standing at the edge of the practice field. "That was quite the show."

He sounded impressed but wry at the same time, as if he hadn't expected us to topple that set of targets, but he couldn't bring himself to find the act all that amazing either. I touched down on the grass, my feet braced against the earth and muscles still humming with adrenaline, trying to ignore the pinch of annoyance.

No one had insisted he stick around and watch our continued training to perfect our combined attacks. If he was bored with it, he could go jerk himself off with his one hand.

"Considering your areas of expertise," Loki said from behind me, "I'd expect you to know the difference between warfare and entertainment." His voice had the same edge I'd heard yesterday when he'd talked to Tyr. If anything, after a couple hours of performing with that additional spectator, the edge was even more prominent.

Also like yesterday, Tyr ignored him. "You do seem to run out of targets quickly," he remarked in Thor's general direction. Then he turned to Freya. "What part are we meant to play in the battle exactly while this bunch is demonstrating their flashy talents?"

"I'm sure we'll fight beside them as always," Freya said, her expression suggesting she wasn't incredibly fond of Tyr's attitude either. "We just need to make sure to give them room to work those talents. I've seen them in a real skirmish too. It really is incredible the way their magic merges."

"And if that doesn't suit you, we already know you make excellent bait," Loki tossed in.

Tyr did stiffen at that remark. He frowned at the group of us. "I came back because I understood my help was wanted. I'm here to protect Asgard. Is that a problem?"

"Of course not, of course not," Thor said, stepping forward.

"Come now," Loki said. "You know me. I always enjoy a good joke. Don't be so quick to draw arms." The tension in his posture told a different story. He bent to scoop up an apple that had inadvertently ended up in the jumble of targets we'd hauled out to the field, tossed it in his hand, and caught it. "Let me know when we're set up for another go. I feel the need to stretch my legs."

He sauntered off past the nearest halls without another word or a backward glance, still tossing the apple with sharp flicks of his wrist. My gaze caught Baldur's. He gave me a pained smile as if to say, *I suppose it could be worse?*

I wasn't really sure it could be, though. Every time I'd seen Loki in the last few days, he'd seemed more irritable and more distant at the same time.

"We could get carting those new targets over," Hod said.

He turned his face toward me, including me as well as his twin in the suggestion, but the tug in my gut pulled me toward the slim figure just vanishing beyond the gleaming buildings. "I think I'd better try to talk to him," I said.

Hod didn't need to ask me who. "Good luck," he said, not entirely sarcastically.

I hurried away from them in the direction Loki had gone, letting some of my valkyrie strength and speed flow through my legs. I'd never beat Loki in a race, but he wasn't walking that fast. I got the impression he hadn't expected anyone to bother following him.

"Does the great Tyr request my presence?" he asked when I caught up, his gaze still fixed on the forest he was heading toward.

"No," I said, abruptly annoyed with him. "What's with you lately? He's kind of a jerk, but he's not *that* bad."

"Perhaps he should be the one you're chatting with then."

I restrained a growl of frustration. As I strode faster to keep pace with him, a hint of scent drifted off his shirt. A tinge of that sulfuric smell I associated with Muspelheim. Had he gone back there again this morning?

My irritation washed away with a wave of hopelessness. I gritted my teeth against the sensation. Loki had given me a whole new life, had seen me as worthy of it when none of the other gods would have looked twice at me. I couldn't give up on him.

A spark of inspiration hit me with the leap of the apple up from his palm. I walked alongside him a few steps farther, and then I launched myself into the air just as he tossed the fruit. With a whip of my arm, my fingers had closed around its smooth skin.

"Pixie!" Loki said in protest.

I whirled around to face him, hovering a couple feet above the ground with a flutter of my wings, and tossed the apple like he had. "You want it back? Come and get it."

Even a grouchy Loki couldn't resist a little mischief. A gleam lit in his amber eyes. "Are you sure that's a dare you want to make?" he said in the sly tone I was more used to.

I arched an eyebrow at him. "Trying to talk me out of it because you're afraid I'll win?"

He sprang at me without warning, but not at full-speed—and I'd been waiting for a move like that anyway. With a sweep of my wings, I took off toward the forest. My fingers stayed clutched around the apple. It was an ordinary one, already bruised from being tumbled with the practice supplies, but right then it felt like something precious.

The breeze warbled as Loki dashed after me. I veered one way and swooped another, pushing my wings as fast as they would carry me. Once I was in the shelter of the forest, he'd have a harder time pouncing.

There. I shot between two trees on the fringes, jerking to the side an instant before his hand could close around my ankle. Indignant laughter escaped his lips. He wove back and forth through the brush, never more than a few feet behind me. Then, just as I reached the point where the wilder forest gave way to the apple orchard, he sprang so fast I didn't even feel him coming until his arm had already snagged my waist.

The sudden tug spun me around as we fell. My wings contracted into my back. Loki's arm jerked up, his hand cupping the back of my head to protect me from the worst of the impact as we crashed into the soft grass at the edge of the orchard. Which meant he landed over me, his heave of breath spilling hot against my cheek, his lips just inches from mine, his body braced above me.

Even though his arms had caught most of his weight, panic jolted through me at the impression of being pinned down by his body. My back tensed against Loki's protective embrace. His playful expression vanished.

He pushed himself backward, moving off me as he slid his arm free, and a different sort of panic flashed through me. I was about to lose him again, to lose the pleased light I'd just reignited in him.

My hand darted out to snag in the fabric of his tunic, halting him. "No."

Loki peered down at me, going completely still. "Ari?"

I inhaled shakily. Too many emotions were colliding inside me. The fact that it terrified me that I might lose him terrified me all over again in turn. When had anything or anyone other than Petey mattered to me even half this much?

If this scenario went wrong, where the hell would that leave me?

I didn't know, but I did know that it'd be even worse not to have Loki at all. I adjusted my grip on his shirt, willing my breaths to even out. One of his knees had brushed my inner thigh when he'd moved. My skin was already tingling from that contact.

He wouldn't hurt me. He wouldn't take anything other than what I offered him. I knew *that*.

"I want this," I said, holding his gaze. "I trust you."

Loki flinched. I couldn't have said what reaction I'd expected, but it definitely hadn't been that. My heart ached before he even spoke.

"You'd be the first, then," he said, and hesitated. "I don't want to stir up those memories, to make you think of... I'm not very good at handling fragile objects, pixie. I have a tendency of breaking them, even if I end up fixing them after."

The rawness in his voice made my heart beat even faster, but it was a heady drumming now. My initial panic was pulling back, bit by bit, in the wake of the warmth between our bodies.

"Maybe you just think you're not good with them because no one ever expected you to be before," I said.

Loki stared at me. "Ari," he said, and then didn't seem to know how to continue.

I tugged on his shirt. "Anyway, I don't break that easily."

A hoarse chuckle slipped from his lips. His head dipped down, his nose grazing mine. "No, you certainly don't."

I tipped my face, seeking out his mouth, and he closed that last short distance in an instant. His lips met mine with a flicker of heat that coursed straight down to my core. He kept himself braced over me, no part of us touching except our mouths and that knee resting just above my own.

That kiss bled into another and another, each one a little deeper, a little sweeter. The nerves still keeping my muscles tight started to loosen. My fingers stayed curled in the fabric of Loki's shirt, but the rest of me relaxed against the grassy ground. This was nothing at all like those memories he'd alluded to. It was something utterly different. Something new.

Loki eased a little closer, his hips pressing against mine ever so slightly, and my pulse hiccupped. But his tongue teased into my mouth at the same moment, and the fear was overshadowed by that fresh rush of heat.

Our tongues tangled like dancing flames. I dropped the apple I'd still been holding with my other hand and looped my arm behind Loki's neck to pull him even closer.

He shifted his weight onto one arm so he could stroke his fingers along the curve of my breast. A gentle stream of heat followed his touch. I arched toward him, kissing him harder, wanting more.

The trickster eased his lips away from mine to consider my tank top. His finger glided along the neckline, sparking pleasure across my collarbone.

"What should we do with this?" he murmured.

"Whatever you want," I said with a tickle of curiosity to see where he'd take that opening.

A grin curled his mouth. "Hmm. You do have a decent supply of clothing in that hall of yours, don't you?"

"Yes?" I said, giving him a questioning look. Freya and I had taken a brief trip down to their house in Midgard not long after we'd first arrived so I could collect some changes of clothes.

"Excellent. In that case..."

He traced a line down my breastbone, and literal flames leapt up in the wake of his finger. The magical sear of them soaked into my skin without burning. They spread across my top, consuming the fabric as they went, flooding me with more and more of that blissful heat. When they licked across my now-bare nipples, I gasped with a bolt of pleasure.

I yanked Loki's mouth back to mine. As he kissed me, the flames he'd lit continued their scorching path down— over my ribcage and across my belly, tickling my navel, then creeping along the waist of my jeans.

When they sizzled over my clit, my hips arched of their own accord. The flood of pleasure was so intense my whole body shook. A moan caught in my throat, and my teeth nicked Loki's lip. "Loki..."

"Right here, pixie," he murmured. "Whatever you need from me." His thumb flicked over the peak of my breast, drawing a whimper out of me.

I ran my hands down his lean chest. His flames

hadn't even singed his own clothes. I grasped the hem and yanked it up. "Off."

He stripped off the tunic and tossed it to the side in the blink of an eye. I'd already reached lower to cup his rigid cock through his slacks. Loki groaned, and the flames he'd sent right down to my feet a few moments ago returned to lick across my core. The gentle but hot caress brought another moan to my lips. As he leaned in to reclaim my mouth, I felt as if I were being devoured in both places at once.

My hips bucked again, brushing the bulge of his arousal. I fumbled with his fly. There was no hesitation, no fear left in me, only a torrent of desire.

More flames sparked as Loki kicked off the rest of his clothes. They crackled across my nipples and nibbled my throat, blazed across my belly and lapped at my clit. Not a hint of pain came with the thrill they provoked.

The sensations coursed deeper when Loki teased the head of his cock along my opening. I made an insistent sound and raised my legs to embrace his hips. He slid into me with a surge of heat and pleasure. A sigh tumbled from my lips.

Loki eased in and out of me slowly, ecstasy swelling within me with each stroke of his cock, filling me with the most delicious burn. The magical flames tingling over every sensitive spot on my body had me writhing with just a few thrusts. One pinched my clit, and the dam inside me broke. I came, shuddering, on a wave of bliss.

"Oh, I think we can take you further than that," Loki said by my ear. He kissed me through the final tremors, and then he started moving again, his thrusts still measured but picking up speed. With each one he filled me deeper. That sizzling heat spread across my whole sex, pulsing against my clit, making my body flare hotter inside and out.

Another wave of pleasure built and built, until I was trembling for release. Whimpers escaped me with every panted breath. My fingers tangled in the silky hair at the back of Loki's head. He met my eyes, his amber eyes smoldering with a strange softness as he gazed down at me. We rocked together, every plunge of his cock bringing a bolt of bliss. His expression tensed with his own rising need.

"Come with me, Ari," he said, in the most tender voice I'd ever heard from him. The flames licked at me with a sharper prickling of pleasure, but it was that tone and the look in his eyes that sent my spirit flying.

I cried out, my head tipping back as my eyes rolled up, my back bowing to ride the explosion of my second release. Heat burst in my core and radiated through me. A ragged cry escaped Loki in turn. He thrust harder, gripping my thigh, and I spiraled even higher than before. For an instant, as his hips jerked and he followed me, my vision blurred with a white-hot glaze of ecstasy.

Loki swayed to a stop over me. He held there for several seconds as he caught his breath, and then he slipped his arm under me, flipping us in one smooth movement so he was on his back holding me against his chest.

I snuggled against him, still drifting back down from the heights of my orgasm. His fiery heat had seared the sweat from our bodies, but my skin was flushed everywhere it touched his.

The trickster's fingers brushed over my hair. I nuzzled his jaw and lifted my head for another kiss. His hand rose to cup my jaw, and the kiss lingered on and on until I was breathless again. My heart thumped so giddily that I couldn't think of what to say.

Loki tucked his head against mine. "No proclamations?" he said lightly, but I thought I caught a hint of longing in his tone.

I swallowed thickly, breathing in the spicy scent of his skin. "Did you have one to make?

"You know, I think I just might."

I wasn't prepared for the rush of emotion that hit me, even though he hadn't actually said anything yet: an answering affection—and a jolt of fear at what might happen when this moment ended and we were faced with all the horrible complications of real life again. I wrapped my arm around his chest, hugging him tight. The words slipped out before I could catch them.

"Don't leave."

"Whoever said I was going to?" Loki replied, but his muscles had tensed against me, just slightly.

"You've been going down to Muspelheim," I said to his chest. "I can smell it on you. But you didn't tell the rest of us about it. You've been talking to Surt?"

He really tensed then, his body shifting as if to propel himself upright and push me back from him. "If you think for one second I'd align myself with that wretched excuse for a—"

"No!" I caught his shoulder, drawing back far enough

to hold his gaze. "That's not what I meant. I know you. I know you wouldn't turn your back on us because you wanted to. I was just worried that Odin was sending you off on some new scheme. Forcing you to play one of his games. He pushed you so far before..." My grip on Loki's shoulder tightened, as if I could hold him with me, away from the Allfather and his manipulations, just with that one hand.

Loki's expression softened in an instant. He did sit up, but only to collect me against him, hugging me on his lap. "Oh, pixie. You don't need to worry about that. My blood oath with Odin still connects us, but any compulsion to obey his orders dissolved with our first deaths. I don't intend to follow his instructions into villainy ever again."

"Then what *have* you been doing down there? You've seemed... upset, the last few days. And the way you've been going at Tyr—"

"Tyr is a different story," Loki muttered. "Do you know how he lost his hand?"

I hesitated, suddenly not sure I wanted to know. "I don't."

"I told you they chained up my wolfish son. He was a smart one. He could tell they weren't just playing games like they told him, testing his strength. When they brought the dark elf-made chain, he wouldn't let them put it on him unless one of the gods was willing to offer his hand in Fenrir's mouth as a show of good faith." Loki let out a humorless chuckle. "Tyr was the one 'brave' enough to offer. Without any faith. And so he lost his hand, and my son lost his freedom for the rest of his life."

"Oh. No wonder you don't like him."

He sighed. "I suppose I should be over those grudges by now. It's just been the last week, so many memories stirred up..."

"I know," I said gently.

He tucked my head under his, his embrace tightening. "About the rest—my little jaunts down to Muspelheim... Surt came to me offering an alliance. I played along for a little while to see what I could find out about his plans and resources."

"And you went with him into his realm to discuss all that?" I leaned into him to ease the prickling of fear. "What if he'd tried to cage you like he did with Odin?"

Loki made a dismissive sound. "Do you really think any regular giant could outwit me? I stayed on my guard. Unfortunately, *he* didn't trust me particularly, although I suppose in this case that caution was warranted. I was hoping to have more to report before I spoke to the rest of you. I'm not sure anything I gleaned will be all that useful."

"Are you going back?"

"It would appear not. This morning he insisted that we'd done enough talking, that I commit myself to his cause in unshakeable fashion. I don't think he was very pleased when I told him I wasn't satisfied with my end of the theoretical bargain." His next chuckle sounded more like his usual self.

"You've been grouchy since before Tyr showed up," I said. "Were you just frustrated that you hadn't been able to find out more from Surt?"

"Well, yes. That, and..." Loki paused, his chest rising

and falling with a slow breath. "Talking with him, it reminded me too much of certain feelings that used to be all too much a part of my life. Feelings that had been creeping back into my mind, in ways I hadn't totally acknowledged."

"What do you mean?"

"I have many real grievances with the gods of Asgard, pixie, but—I didn't have to agree to Odin's terms. I didn't have to keep his secrets. There were parts of me that enjoyed seeing the gods get their comeuppance at my hands. Who's to say whether I might have fit in more smoothly over time if it wasn't for that?" He sighed. "Perhaps I'm not the monster they liked to see me as, but I'm not a hero by any stretch of the imagination either."

My chest squeezed. I buried my face in the crook of his neck. "You're you," I said. "Who's a hero all of the time anyway?"

I certainly wasn't. But I'd be damned if anyone, king of the gods or giant with flaming sword or army of draugr, took the joys and peace I'd found in my new life away from me.

"I'm honored by your devotion," Loki said. His tone was dry, but his embrace tightened around me for a moment before he eased back. "I suppose if we want to get on with the heroic side of things, we should find out what the others have gotten up to. Back to that bloody training."

I got up, looking around as he pulled his slacks back on. "Um," I said, crossing my arms over my bare chest. "I do have plenty of clothes back in my hall. I don't suppose you had a plan for how I'd make it *back* to my hall to get them, now that you've turned what I had on into ash?"

Loki laughed and tossed his tunic to me. "Wear this. I can protect your modesty as well as the rest of you."

The shirt was long even on Loki's tall frame. On me it fell nearly to my knees. I stuck my tongue out at him as we set off for the city.

"How do you know it won't be *me* protecting you, huh?"

He grinned, his hand dipping down to close around mine. "I'll be perfectly happy either way."

22

Aria

"Are we sure this is the best course of action, after everything we've learned?" Hod said as the group of us came down off the rainbow bridge.

The humid air in the part of Midgard that Loki had directed us to closed in around us. The dark god turned his head, presumably taking in the sounds and feel of the terrain around us just like I was taking in the look of it. Jungle-like vegetation grew tangled along one side of the road. A cluster of small houses on stilts stood in the distance in the other direction.

"We don't need to decide how to *act* yet," Loki said, brushing his hands together. "At this point, we're simply investigating. One of the draugr I convinced Surt to show me had a shirt with a very specific logo. It's almost certain that victim was picked up around here, which means there must be another gateway in this area, whether the dark elves are still delivering bodies through it or not."

I stretched out my wings behind me. "Let's go find out. We can't help them fix their realm until they've stopped hurting all kinds of innocent people."

"If we catch them in the act..." Thor muttered, hefting his hammer as we started walking. He didn't need to finish that threat.

Baldur came up beside me. "Can you sense their energy nearby?" he asked.

I'd already pushed my awareness forward across the terrain. "I might need to go up in the air to get a wider impression—oh." A shimmering clot of that oily energy brushed my valkyrie senses from what felt like not far at all to our right. "There are dark elves that way," I said, pointing into the jungle. "Four or five of them, I think."

"Into the wilds it is, then," Loki said with a spring in his step. Our encounter by the orchard seemed to have released him from the bad mood that'd been gripping him for so long.

Thor bashed a path with his hammer for a couple paces until the trickster pointed out that "it might be preferable if they didn't hear us coming from miles away." After that, we picked our way across the damp ground, around tree trunks choked with vines, much more slowly. But we'd only been heading that way for a few minutes when a figure appeared amid the brush in front of us: a dark elf, short and stout like most of them were, with the usual black hair and sallow skin. He held up a white cloth just a few shades lighter than his hand like a gesture of surrender.

We halted, studying him. "You've been stealing people from the towns near here," Thor rumbled. "We need to—"

"We don't want to continue those crimes," the elf broke in. "Not if there are other ways. We've had delegations waiting at our remaining gateways, watching for you to come for us again. There's no way for us to reach out to you in Asgard on our own."

"A delegation?" Hod asked, his tone wary but not harsh.

"Three of my superiors would return with you to Asgard to speak with Odin," the man said. "Between them they have authority over several sectors of Nidavellir, and they could persuade the other leaders too if they feel it's in our interests. We would rather this conflict didn't turn to outright war."

The five of us exchanged a glance. A delegation wanting to discuss peace with Odin—that sounded promising. It was kind of hard to take them completely at face value after everything we'd already seen, though.

"Have these 'superiors' come out," Loki suggested with a beckoning motion. "We'll want to look them over. If we're to trust them, we need to see no weapons and none of your war-like contraptions."

The dark elf bobbed his head and shuffled away through the dense vegetation. Less than a minute later, he returned with three companions—two men and a woman, all of them similar in stature and coloring but wearing embroidered tunics in a deep blue that I guessed reflected their status among the elves.

"I can look them over," Hod volunteered with a wry

smile. He lifted his hand, and his shadows stirred around him. They seeped through the bushes around us to coil around the dark elves, testing their pockets and any bagginess in their clothes for hidden items.

"We don't want to fight," the woman said. "We're only trying to do right by our people."

"You lost the benefit of the doubt when you started slaughtering a whole raft of other people to do that," Loki retorted. "Give us a moment to confer."

We took a couple of steps back, and Loki swept his arm with a tingle of magic that must have concealed us the way he'd hidden me when we'd gone to watch over Petey.

"From what I could sense of their motives, they're mostly anxious about the future and a little desperate for this attempt to work out," Baldur said softly. "There was hope in them, and regret for the past. I think they honestly want to bargain with us. I felt no sense of deception."

"That's the same impression I got from them," I said. "That doesn't mean we shouldn't keep a close watch. But this could be the way we beat Surt for good, if we bring the dark elves over to our side, couldn't it?"

Thor was frowning. "I'm not sure how far I'd trust the dirt-eaters to follow through on any agreement after everything they've already done. We may not need them."

"It certainly can't hurt to *have* them," Loki put in. "In my opinion, we may as well hear what they have to say before we go dismissing it."

"I agree," Hod said. "They've done horrible things,

but they were in a horrible situation. And what could the three of them hope to do to us or Odin that they couldn't have when they had him captured for all those years?"

Thor lowered his head. "All right," he said. "But I'm keeping Mjolnir ready."

"As well you should, my friend," Loki said, clapping him on the arm. He waved away the magic he'd drawn around us and raised his voice so it would carry to the dark elves. "All right, come along. Let's see this through quickly."

The three elves trudged through the jungle with us quietly, their expressions stoic. Were those prickles of shame I felt from them for the harm they'd done or also for having to turn to the gods for help at all? I couldn't tell. As long as it was mostly the former, I guessed it didn't matter.

Loki led the way up the rainbow bridge, Baldur beside him and Thor, Hod, and me bringing up the rear behind our "guests." Freya and Tyr had stayed behind in Asgard to continue discussing strategy and catching up, but they were waiting by the top of the bridge. Freya took one look at the dark elves in our midst, and her eyebrows shot up. Her hand leapt to her sword.

"Why are you bringing *them* here?" she demanded.

"A delegation to speak with Odin," Loki said with a sweep of his arm toward our company. "We'll take them straight to him, if you don't mind."

Tyr's expression was skeptical, but he didn't argue. Freya fell into step beside us as we headed down Valhalla's main road. "Are you sure this is quite—"

"What is this?" a low voice demanded, rolling

through the air. Odin had emerged from his hall and was striding toward us faster than I'd have thought that stately body was capable of.

Loki stepped to the side as if he felt the dark elves might as well state their own case. The woman bowed her head to the approaching Allfather. "Great Odin," she said, her shoulders tensed. "We know we have done you and the people of Midgard wrong. If you would give us the chance—"

"Begone!" he said, as thunderous as I'd ever heard Thor, coming to a stop in front of them. "Begone from my sight. Begone from my realm."

Hod stiffened where he'd also eased to the side. "Father, I think we should at least hear them out."

"There is nothing a dark elf could say that would be of any interest to me," Odin said. "No deals can be made with those who act like vermin." He waved them off with a sweep of his cloak. His spear gleamed as he smacked the base of it against the marble tiles. "Off with you. *Now*. Before I decide to send you off in a much more painful fashion."

"Odin," I protested, but the dark elves were already cringing in the wake of his anger. They turned and hustled for the rainbow bridge.

"I really think—" Loki began.

Odin swiveled away from him, toward his hall. "I'm not interested in your thoughts on this matter."

He barreled back to his hall as quickly as he'd come at us, his cloak flapping behind him.

My jaw clenched. No. He was not going to ruin what could be our best chance at winning this war—and getting through it *alive*—because he refused to consider anyone's position other than his own.

I darted after him, lifting into the air for the speed my wings could lend me. Odin marched into his hall and flung the door shut behind him with a dull thud. I wrenched it open with a heave of my valkyrie strength and followed.

"Stop!" I said. "We've got to call them back. You've got to talk with them. If we had them on our side—"

He spun back to face me, his single eye so furious my words caught in my throat. "They mean nothing," he said with a jab of his finger. "Did you not hear a single thing I said to you yesterday? We will not suffer the excuses of traitors or lift them up when they will play no part in our victory or failure."

"You don't know they won't," I protested. The door rasped over the floor behind me, footsteps tapping against the floor as at least a couple of the other gods came in behind me. "All you know is we're important. They could make some difference still, couldn't they? The difference between it being an easy victory or a hard one. A difference between whether your own *sons* live or die."

"They held me in a *cage* for years," Odin retorted. "I will not bargain with them."

"*Surt* held you in a cage," I said. "They were following his orders because they didn't know what else to do."

"Because you abandoned them," Loki spoke up, appearing at my left, his arms folded against his chest. He glanced back at the others who'd followed us. "We all did.

The realms are failing because of our neglect. So who can say where the fault lies first?"

"This is the hand we've been dealt," Odin said. "I've seen how it plays out. I've seen all I need to know. For ages I have led you, and Asgard has prospered."

"The other realms matter too," Hod said quietly, coming up at my right.

Odin's eye flashed. "Things will be as they are. We act where we can. There isn't—"

I was so tired of arguing with him. So tired of it going nowhere. All that frustration tore through me at once, and before I'd thought it through, my body was moving. I threw myself at him.

Odin was a god of war, but he wasn't the warrior Thor was—and he hadn't fought anyone in all those years. His spear hand swung around fast enough, but my reflexes reacted faster. I shoved the pole away with my heel and whipped around behind the Allfather before his other snatching hand could catch hold of my limbs. My switchblade leapt into my hand at a tug of my fingers. I grasped Odin's grizzled hair and slammed the knife straight toward his remaining eye.

My hand jerked to a stop less than an inch from piercing the brown iris. Odin had gone rigid. The hall around us was silent. When I didn't follow through with the blow, he shifted to shake me from his shoulders, but I was already springing off him. I landed on the floor right in front of him, glaring up at him, the switchblade still gleaming in my grip.

"If I'd wanted things to turn out that way, you'd have no eyes now," I said. "You'd see nothing except for those 'whispers and fragments' in your head. Did they warn you about that? Did you see me coming? Or is it possible there's a thing or two that you miss?"

Odin stared down at me, his jaw working. A light touch fell on my shoulder. To my surprise, it was Baldur's clear voice that rang out.

"She's right, father. You don't know everything. We all should have a say in how we fight this war—in everything we do from here on."

Odin blinked at him. "My son."

Baldur swallowed audibly, but he didn't back down. "You've ruled us well. I love you. But I will not stand beside you if you push every other opportunity we have away. The rest of us have lived almost as long as you now. We've seen almost as much—we've seen things you haven't. These are our lives, maybe the last we'll ever get. We should have as much of a say in how we use them as you do."

I looked up at the light god, startled by the vehemence in his voice. Baldur's sparkling gaze was fixed on Odin, his stance firm. With the murmur of other footsteps, I felt four other figures come to stand around us.

"You've done enough," Hod said. "No more lies, no more schemes behind our backs. We deserve that much respect."

"We *all* have ideas we can contribute," Thor said. "We can't get anywhere if you won't listen to anyone but yourself. If you're hiding things from us."

Odin's gaze slid to someone now just behind me. "You told them," he said hollowly.

"I showed them," Loki said in a low voice. "The circumstances demanded it. And don't you think it was time?"

"It was." Freya walked up to her husband, setting her hand on his arm. "Share the burden with us, love. Let us construct this new path together. The rest... The rest we can discuss when the catastrophe is averted."

Odin's shoulders sagged slightly. He exhaled in a rush. "I know what I have seen," he said, but his tone faltered more than it had before.

We had to press this advantage while we had it. "We can call back the dark elves," I said. "Or—if you don't want to deal with them, let one of your sons talk to them. You..." The answer came to me as soon as I started to put it to words. "You need to make your peace with Muninn. She doesn't like Surt. She doesn't want his war either. But whatever happened between the two of you, she can't get past it, not without some offering from you. She was one of your closest companions for centuries, wasn't she? There has to be some way you can win her back."

Odin grimaced, and I expected him to argue. Then he lowered his head and ran his hand over his beard.

"I may know a way to reach out to her," he said. "But you must bring her to me first. I will not meet her on Surt's ground while he still rules."

23

Hod

"They might be angry after the way Odin chased their three leaders off," Ari said as we crossed the field toward Valhalla. The grass was getting taller, the soft spears hissing against our feet. I dragged in a deep lungful of its warm near-sweet scent, as if it could last me the entire time I was in the dark elves' caves.

"We already know Muninn has more than enough anger toward Odin and the rest of us," I pointed out. "I'm not sure your request will be any more welcome."

"Mostly Odin," Ari muttered. "And there's only one of her."

"And she trapped us in a nearly inescapable prison for longer than I care to remember." I reached out with enough sense of her presence to rumple the waves of her hair. "I think we should just say that both of us are heading into a fair bit of danger. There's no winning the contest of who should be most concerned, valkyrie."

"Maybe not. I'm still going to worry, though." She was silent for a moment. Then, so quickly I almost stumbled, she turned and wrapped her arms around me, stopping me with her embrace.

"Ari?" I said, surprised even if I was pleased at the same time. Norns knew our valkyrie could be tender, but I wouldn't have expected this much affection out of the blue.

My arms came around her, hugging her to me. I couldn't deny I'd have preferred to never let her go, for neither of us to have needed to venture off into uncertain realms.

"I just... You know how much you mean to me, don't you?" she said. "You and the others... You mean so much to me that it scares me. But I told myself, I *promised* myself, that I wasn't going to let myself back down out of fear anymore. You have to know—in the last ten years, no one's mattered as much to me except Petey, and you've seen how much I care about him."

"I have," I said, my voice becoming hoarse. "You don't need to say anything, Ari. I'm not waiting for something you haven't given me. The way you are, right now—that's all I want. I swear it. All right?"

She nodded against my shoulder, but she was still holding onto me so tightly it made my stomach knot—for her, for how hard she tried to do right by everyone, for how hard it was for her to accept that she might be loved as she was. I didn't think I could have loved her more, and those feelings had nothing to do with what she said or didn't say.

I brought my hand to the side of her face and eased her into a kiss. She might not have initiated it, but the moment my lips brushed hers, she claimed my mouth, pouring so much passion into our linked bodies that a bolt of desire shot through my chest to my groin.

Later. When this was over, when Surt was conquered, we'd have all the time in the realms to explore each other further than we already had.

The walk through Valhalla was becoming increasingly familiar. I only needed a few brief tendrils of shadow to make my steady way between the rows of tables now. A hint of a chill emanated from the hearth, the doorway beyond it at odds with its normal purpose. Ari stepped through onto Yggdrasil's path first and waited for me to join her.

"Let's see who can make it back first," she said, sounding more relaxed as we started across the trunk.

"I'm not sure this is the right time to have a race," I said.

"Okay, maybe not. Just—be careful with them, all right? We don't know how much we can trust them."

"The same to you with Muninn."

"Oh, believe me, I'll be watching my step around her for a long time, no matter how this pans out." She stopped at the branching that emitted the acrid smell of Muspelheim and squeezed my hand. "I'll see you soon."

Somehow that casual promise released a little of my distress at knowing she was venturing off into Surt's realm yet again. "And I'll see you," I said.

She kissed me quickly, and then she was darting down the branch.

I didn't have to walk much farther to reach the route I needed to take. I squared my shoulders and strode along the branch to the gate that would take me to Nidavellir.

The air that washed over me on the other side was as damp and chilly as before. I tested my footing on the rocky floor and turned my head to where the guards had been waiting last time. I doubted they changed up their preferred post much.

"I come from Odin with an urgent need to speak to any of your leaders."

The guards murmured amongst themselves without even bothering to address me this time. It sounded as though they were having something of a disagreement, but I couldn't make out enough words to put together the content of it. I waited it out, shifting from one foot to the other and hoping my discomfort wasn't apparent.

Finally, one of them moved toward me, a shift in the dank air. "You can follow me? Come on, then. I can't promise how much he'll want to see you, though."

"Whatever you can do," I said with a grateful dip of my head.

My shadows helped me trace the path of my dark elf guide with only an occasional stubbed toe on the uneven patches in the cave floor. I hadn't been through here often enough to have formed much of a mental map, but I had the impression we were going the same way as before. That impression was reinforced when I stepped out into a larger room that felt the same as the one where I'd met the local commander on my first visit.

"Wait here," the dark elf instructed.

For the first few minutes, I wondered why he'd left me unguarded. Then a soft scuffing sound down the tunnel behind me told me that wasn't the case—he simply hadn't drawn my attention to my sentinel.

It seemed like longer than the last time that I waited. Perhaps the commander didn't want to be bothered with me this time. When footsteps finally scraped against the stone floor to meet me, there was a sharpness to them I didn't remember.

His voice was sharp too. "Blind One. So you return. What is it this time? I've already had word that your Allfather ran a peaceful delegation out of Asgard this morning. I don't see what's to gain from talking now."

"I understand that," I said quickly. "And I apologize for the way your comrades were treated. Odin is still recovering from his imprisonment, and I hope you can understand why he wouldn't have the most pleasant associations with the dark elves right now. But the rest of us believe we should at least attempt a treaty. He's come to agree with that stance. That's why I'm here."

"Am I supposed to just take your word for it that the Allfather has changed his mind so quickly?"

I dipped my hand into my pocket and held out a carved stone token. "He gave me this as proof that I'm here in his stead, speaking for him."

One of the commander's underlings, I suspected, slunk forward and snatched the stone from my fingers. There was a minute of silence as the commander considered it.

Odin didn't give out those signs of his favor easily. He

imbued the runes on them with a temporary magical glow that only he could create, that should tell anyone who saw it that it had come from the Allfather himself, and recently. Of course, that didn't mean the dark elves had to accept it as proof.

"Your delegation was waiting for us," I said. "They had something specific they wanted to offer. I'll hear that offer now, if you'll let me. I can negotiate on Odin's behalf. We don't want to see this realm fail, I can promise you that."

A rough breath escaped the commander. He flicked the token back at me—it struck my arm and tapped to the ground. I bent to pick it up, my heart sinking at the same time.

"What if we no longer believe in anything you'd promise?" the commander said.

I hesitated, and it occurred to me that talking might not be enough. It hadn't been enough to break through to Odin. How could it be to shatter the centuries of animosity that must have built up as we'd ignored the outer realms?

"I can show you," I said, hoping I was right. "You can see me make good on that promise right before your eyes. Take me to one of the caves that's starting to crumble."

The commander exchanged a few words with his underlings. Then he sighed. "All right. Come along then."

He didn't slow his pace for me or offer any assistance, but that was fine. I kept up well enough as they led me deeper into the warren of caves. A mild claustrophobia prickled over my skin, but I pushed aside my uneasiness. How much worse was it to live in this place all the time and not know when the ceiling might fall on your head?

"Here," the commander said, drawing to a halt. One of his underlings grasped my sleeve and tugged me forward.

My hand came to rest on the edge of an entrance where another cave split off from the wider passage we were standing in. Even in that brief touch, a shiver ran over my palm. This rock was shifting, thinning—minutely but enough to make anyone wary.

"So? What great godly magic will you work?"

I ignored the skepticism in the commander's voice, training all my attention on the cave ahead of me. My shadows flowed from my body along the floor, walls and ceiling, relaying information back to me about every dip and crack. And there were several cracks, spidering along the ceiling and the upper walls. I set my jaw and bowed my head.

All this dark rock, this cold mass all around us—it resonated with part of my nature, deep down. I focused on the cracks I could feel almost as clearly as if I were grazing my fingertips over them, pouring more and more shadow into them. Letting that shadow flow on up into the solid rock. Trickling through every gap, every unsteady space. Hardening, solidifying, as cold and firm as mid-winter's ice.

Pouring all that cool energy through me left my lungs clenching. I sucked in a breath and propelled more forward. I had to do everything I could. I had to ensure not one pebble dropped from this ceiling in the following days, or everything I'd attempted here would be for naught.

I wasn't sure how much time had passed before sending forth more shadows sent a splinter of pain through my chest. I eased back, letting the last few wafts of darkness test my handiwork.

The rock all along the narrow passage was smooth now, every crevice sealed. It held firm against my resting hand. I turned back to the commander.

He brushed past me, the closest he'd dared to come to me so far, and stalked into the cave. His feet stilled. He turned, stopped, and turned again. His fingers whispered over the stone surface.

"This isn't an illusion?" he said, but his voice was already awed. "It'll hold?"

"Better than any rock you've ever dealt with," I said.

"It's not enough to fix all our troubles. Not by far."

"I know." I inhaled deeply into my aching lungs. "I would come back. Once a week, until such a time as we decided a different arrangement would be better. I'd stay long enough to stabilize another passage like this, or to help clear new caves, or simply to hear your news and pass on any I have myself."

The commander returned to the mouth of the passage. "You must have conditions of your own, from Odin."

"You will cut off all relations with Surt," I said. "Barricade any gateways to his realm—I can help you with that. Pass on what information you know of his army and his schemes. You didn't really want to be his lackeys anyway, did you?"

"If we do that now, how can we trust that you'll follow through on your end? You might defeat Surt tomorrow, and where does that leave us if you renege?"

I held up my hand, my heart starting to thud. I'd come down here knowing I might need to take things this far. I'd been prepared for it. But my body still balked for a moment before I could force out the words.

"I'll take a blood oath. Like the one that bound Odin and Loki for all of their first lives. Neither I nor the one who swears with me will be able to back down from that."

A hush fell over the dark elves gathered around me that felt more startled than before. The commander swallowed audibly. "A blood oath with a dark elf?"

"We failed you too long," I said. "I think you're owed this much."

"Well... Come with me, then. It isn't me you should be swearing to. I'll tell them what I saw. If you're truly willing to go through with this—you'll have our loyalty, however much of it you require."

24

Aria

I perched on the edge of the table, my feet braced against the bench as I resisted the urge to swing them impatiently. The faded mead smell of Valhalla seemed thicker than usual today, although maybe that was just because Odin was sitting on his golden throne where I'd first pictured him, before I'd known the real god.

"She said she would come," I said, pressing my hands against the varnished wood to stop them from fidgeting too. "But she couldn't just hop back here the way I can. She would have had to get to the portal in Surt's fortress." My gaze shot to the Allfather. "You *did* make sure Yggdrasil's magic would open to her, didn't you?"

He inclined his head, his eye glinting at my skepticism. "As I promised. I never closed it to her. A being of Asgard stays a being of Asgard."

That was one small relief. I didn't think Muninn had

tried to return in however long it'd been since she and Odin had first gone their separate ways.

She'd been watching for me, or for anyone from Asgard, like before. I hadn't gone far from the gate I'd entered Muspelheim through this time—just giving myself enough distance from the guarding dragon that I hadn't been too worried it'd swoop down on me. Then I'd simply sat at the base of the cliff and spread out the cloth I'd brought on the dark rock. White silk, courtesy of Freya—a request for a truce, like the dark elves had shown us.

It had taken about half an hour for Muninn to notice, but she had come. And even though she'd grimaced when I'd told her Odin wanted to speak with her, to make amends, she'd stayed and listened.

"How do I know this isn't a trap?" she'd demanded when I'd finished my plea. "All of you planning revenge for the hand I had in your capture?"

"I guess you can't know for sure," I'd said. "But how can we know you won't pull some kind of memory trick on us either? We're trusting you to come in good faith. I hope you can find a little trust for us too. If you don't like the look of things, you can just leave."

She'd hummed to herself and ruffled her dress, and then she'd said that she would give the Allfather a minute or two, no promises of more. "The gate to Asgard from here is with the others in the back of Surt's fortress," she'd said. "He's given me free access to them, but I may need to wait until there's no one around to see which I take."

"Of course," I'd said. "We'll be waiting."

And now here we were.

"Even if she doesn't come, we can win this battle without her," Hod said from where he was sitting on the bench next to me. He rested a reassuring hand on my calf. "The dark elves have given us a good starting point. Thor is seeing what he can make of his scheme with the giants."

"Thor the Schemer," Loki murmured from where he'd propped himself against the next table over. "I never thought I'd see that day."

"You can't claim *all* the wits in Asgard, trickster," Freya said teasingly. She was standing on the other side of the throne from the hearth, looking as if she thought she might need to defend her husband from his former servant.

Loki grinned. "And I suppose I should be thankful for that."

"How easily can we guard against these illusions of hers?" Tyr asked. He'd taken a sword off the walls, but he let it dangle at his side in a relaxed pose.

"She can't work them on me," Odin said. "I doubt she'd try with me here, but if she did, I'd break you free of them."

"I'll be paying attention to her emotional state," Baldur said. He leaned back against the table where he was sitting next to Loki, his gaze on the hearth. "If I sense any malice, I'll give warning."

"What are you going to say to her?" I asked Odin. Frankly, I was more worried about him screwing this up than anything else. Muninn's feelings about him ran so raw I could see the hurt and rage in her eyes whenever I so much as said his name. If he brought even a hint of his know-it-all arrogance to this conversation, we could kiss any hope of making peace goodbye.

"You'll hear it when I say it to her," the Allfather said evenly, which didn't really comfort me. I shifted my weight, the squirming impulse wriggling deeper through my nerves.

A ripple of energy washed over us from the hearth like a faint breeze. My head jerked up. Odin shifted forward.

"A guest has arrived."

He pulled himself to his feet and considered his spear. After a moment's thought, he leaned it against his throne rather than keeping it in his hand. I guessed even he could figure out that facing Muninn unarmed was going to go over better. Something in his expression softened, more than I'd have thought was possible. Maybe he was really ready for this conversation after all.

A rustling caught my ears, so muted I wasn't sure anyone else except Loki would have caught it. Then a small black shape burst from the hearth and soared toward the ceiling with a fluttering of feathers.

The raven circled beneath the rafters, peering down at us. When she'd glided over our heads a few times—enough to decide we didn't have a bird cage at the ready to toss her into, presumably—she swooped down to land in front of the hearth. She stood up in her human form with the ashy opening at her back. It'd give her a quick escape route if she didn't like what she heard in that minute or two she'd offered us.

"Odin," she said in her softly hoarse voice, her shoulders slightly hunched in a defensive stance. Her large dark eyes shone starkly from her pale face. They didn't leave him for an instant. The rest of us might as well not have been in the room.

"Muninn," Odin said with a respectful dip of his grizzled head. "Thank you for coming. It's been a long time since I saw you here."

"And far too long before that," she shot back.

"Yes." He kept his head low, rubbing his mouth. "I failed to consider that you might want a life of your own beyond what you had serving me. It was an oversight unworthy of me, and I apologize for that."

Muninn blinked, looking startled. Then her mouth tensed again. "And did you only just realize this oversight?"

"It's only recently I've realized just how angry with me you were," Odin said with a hint of irony. "But did you think I forgot about you the moment you set off on your own path? I have looked in on you over the years."

She bristled. "You *spied* on me."

"No!" He raised his hand. "You know my seat doesn't allow me to peer through walls. I didn't invade your privacy. I only caught a glimpse, now and then, when I wanted to be sure of how you were faring. But that was enough to catch a fragment or two of certain types of conversations."

The raven woman was still tensed. Odin let out his breath. "For a long while, I saw you as little more than an extension of myself, and that was wrong. That doesn't mean I wasn't concerned at all with your well-being."

"You had strange ways of showing that concern," she shot back.

A knowing gleam came into his eye. "I never asked anything of you I wasn't completely sure you were capable of handling."

"It's not just me. You've neglected so many of the realms—so many of the people in them—"

"I know," he said. "I have many apologies to make. But we have already started to reach out. We'll bring the strength of the gods back to all the realms."

"I just spoke with the dark elves this morning," Hod put in. He held up his hand, the one marked by a still-raw scratch of a knife that he hadn't let his twin heal. "We'll put things as right as we can. We all should have realized sooner."

Muninn shifted on her feet. She looked from Hod to Odin. "Well, what now? You can't give me back what was lost. How could you possibly make up for all the centuries I was under your thumb?"

The gleam in Odin's eye shone brighter. "I can't make up for them—I acknowledge that. But I *can* give you a little more time with what you most recently lost, and I promise you may make a home for yourself in Asgard or call on us as you need us like any of the gods, without any expectation of your service, from here on."

"What I most recently lost?" the raven woman repeated.

He gave her a smile that looked almost gentle. "I may have missed some very obvious things, but I don't think there's any way I could miss this. I can't summon a spirit for long after this much time detached from the world of the living, but Valhalla has enough power to grant them a brief additional respite."

He lowered his tall frame into his throne, his hands gripping the golden arms. His eye closed. Muninn stared at him, her body rigid.

A faint hum carried through the hall. The hair on the back of my neck rose. I gripped the edge of the table, suppressing a shiver.

There, in front of the throne, three figures started to form. At first they were no more than shadowy impressions, but as Odin's forehead furrowed and the hum rose to a higher pitch, their bodies sharpened. All three were men, one with the coloring of a dark elf but at least half a foot taller than any I'd seen before, one a burly guy with a sweep of light brown hair and soft features that contrasted with his square jaw, and one...

The last one, I recognized. His blond hair had been white when I'd seen him in what I'd assumed was one of Muninn's memories, his face much more lined, but there was no mistaking the scar that cut jaggedly across the left side of his lean face.

In the moment I'd seen, they'd been cuddled together like lovers.

Muninn's eyes had widened. Her hands clenched and opened again at her sides. When the three men had completely solidified, they seemed to come to life. They looked down at themselves and around, the big guy gaping, the dark elf letting out an amused chuckle. Their gazes all settled on the raven woman.

"Svend," she said. "Gunnar. Jerrik. I—"

She cut herself off and simply threw herself at them. In an instant, they'd enveloped her in a joint embrace.

My skin prickled with the feeling that us being here at all was a huge invasion of privacy.

For once, Odin was clearly thinking along the same lines as I was. "We'll give you this time to yourselves," he said quietly, and moved from his throne. All of us who'd assembled there filtered out of the hall of warriors as quickly as our feet would take us.

"How long will those temporary manifestations last?" Loki asked the Allfather when we'd come to a stop on the field outside.

Odin sighed. "Several minutes at least, I hope. It's difficult to summon spirits that long dead back to life, however worthy they may have been. Valhalla's power can only accomplish so much."

"It looked to me as though she was glad to have them at all," Freya said. A soft smile played across the goddess's lips, reminding me that she presided over love as well as war.

A lump had filled my throat. "I think that was the right thing," I said. "To show her—to show her you understood, and that you want her to be happy."

Odin's gaze settled on me for a long moment—long enough that it started to weigh on me. "Perhaps I have needed some reminding to extend the same courtesy to you, my patchwork valkyrie," he said. "I should apologize for that as well."

The apology took me by surprise, but not so much that I forgot myself. "And maybe to your sons and the other gods here as well," I suggested.

He sputtered a chuckle. "You aren't one to back down, are you? We will see how the confrontations ahead of us play out. There will be time enough for more discussions once Surt has been put down. But I am ready to have those discussions."

He glanced at Loki, whose jaw tightened. The trickster god offered a nod of acknowledgment.

It was closer to an hour before Muninn emerged from Valhalla, so I guessed Odin's and the hall's magic had worked better than he'd expected. Or maybe the raven woman had taken some time to herself before rejoining us. A hint of redness lined her eyes and her cheeks were flushed, but her posture was more relaxed than I'd ever seen her before.

"Let's set the realms right," she said. "If you're going to stop Surt from wrecking even more havoc, you need to strike tomorrow afternoon."

25

Aria

The mountainside Muninn had us stop on gave a direct view of Surt's fortress from a distance. She peered at the roughly carved landscape around us and nodded.

"I don't think any of the patrols should catch you here. This isn't along any of their routes. You can wait without any interference until you're ready to jump in."

"Are you sure he's gone?" Hod asked. "The dark elves I spoke with said they'd never seen him leave the fortress. He always seemed to be on guard, watching for a fight."

Muninn's thin lips curled. "For a couple of hours every other afternoon, that Surt is an illusion drawn from their memories. I created a construct of him as part of our arrangement, so that he could go surveying the territories in Midgard where he might begin his invasion. He wanted to give the *appearance* of being constantly on guard."

"There are still guards," I pointed out. Even from across the wide plain between us and the uneven walls, I could make out the figures perched along it and stationed outside the buildings beyond the walls.

The raven woman shrugged. "You're never going to find it *un*guarded. But most of those 'soldiers' have plenty of training and no real battle experience. They'll look to him first before they realize they need to come up with their own plan of defense. If you can sow the destruction you're planning as quickly as you say, you should be able to take out the draugr before they've called many of them up—or started much of any counterattack, really."

"The giants will distract them first," Thor said. "We rush in while they're busy fending off that horde."

"If they show up," Loki said with an arch of his eyebrow.

Thor glowered at him good-naturedly. "They're coming. You should have seen how stirred up they were by the time I was done with my call to action." A little of the light glamor Baldur had cast on him still shone in his hair. I'd never seen him look quite so relieved as when he'd strapped Mjolnir back onto his belt, though.

"We have seven target spots," I said. "Should we look over the map again, now that you all have the fortress to compare?"

"It can't hurt to be as prepared as possible," Baldur said.

Hod pulled out the folded paper he'd been carrying. The dark elves had given it to him: a sketch of the fortress layout with markings to indicate the support walls of the caves they'd helped dig out and expand beneath the surface. They'd confirmed that was where Surt had been stashing his army of the undead—thousands of them now, in vast rows of caverns. If we broke through in just the right spots, we could bring the rocky ceiling toppling down on them all, leaving them as sitting ducks.

Freya and Tyr studied the map again too, even though their job was going to be protecting our backs while the five of us did the heavy work with our combined powers. Odin hadn't been *wrong*, not really. If this worked, it'd be mainly because of the five of us. He just hadn't been completely right either. It might not work at all if it hadn't been for the other ways we'd contributed. If Hod hadn't reached out to the dark elves. If Thor hadn't riled up the giants.

The ledge we were standing on trembled beneath my feet. I tensed where I was crouched. Thor smiled.

"Here they come."

A moment later, the first charge of the giants moved into my line of sight on the plain below. They rushed forward, their heavy feet thundering over the ground, hollering and brandishing their weapons.

Loki rolled his eyes. "You'd think over the ages they might have finally picked up a tiny bit of subtlety."

"The guards are moving," I said. "What if they start bringing the draugr out?"

"Then we send those ones crackling back into the peace of death on the surface," the trickster said.

"We just need all their attention on the giants," Freya said. "The ones by the buildings are heading to the walls now. They're gathering together at the front to watch the approach, just as we expected. Let's go! We can come at them first from the side—they won't know what's hit them until we're already halfway through."

She didn't need to say more than that. We were already pushing off the ledge. Only Muninn hung back, her pale face tight with anxiety for a second before she shifted into her raven form. She flew higher up the mountain, where we'd decided she'd stay and watch to report back to Odin as needed. "Just like old times," she'd said when we'd discussed it, but without too much bitterness.

If this went well, we'd *all* be returning to report to Odin on our success. My pulse thrummed faster as we glided around the edge of the plain and soared toward the fortress's flank. The guards along the wall were shouting at the giants, who'd nearly reached the steaming moat of magma. They *were* bringing up the draugr—several lurching figures had already emerged from a hollow beside one of the buildings. My heart stuttered.

"Hurry," I said. "They're summoning the army."

I flapped my wings even harder than before. Thor surged ahead of us, raising his hammer. We threw ourselves over the stinging heat of the moat, and he let out his battle cry.

I moved automatically now, swinging the short sword I'd grabbed from Valhalla. It might not have the history of my switchblade, but for this battle, I was going in fully armed. Around me, my other gods whipped their magic at the first of our targets, a patch of earth just a few feet from the corner of what looked like barracks.

Fire and light and shadow twined and caught hold of Mjolnir, which smashed into that spot with the force of four gods—and whatever a valkyrie could provide. The ground lurched, and cracks spread across the rocky terrain.

A shout came from the front wall. They knew there was more trouble now. I veered to the right, my wings straining with the effort, and my companions moved with me. We hurtled toward our next target.

With another blast of magic and hammer, the rocky ground all across that side of the fortress's yard shattered inward. The building beside us sagged as the cracks spread beneath its foundations. Gritty dust burst upward with the collapse. I swiped at my eyes, yanking myself around.

"This way!" Freya called, her sword gleaming as she jabbed it ahead of her.

As we sped around the building toward the back of the fortress grounds, pounding footsteps approached. I dodged the shriek of a crossbow bolt and ducked beneath a searing flame flung from one of Surt's magicked blades. The top of my wing stung where the magic grazed it. Thor shouted again, and we propelled our united force at the motley crew of guards who'd left the giants to tackle us.

The smack of the gods' magic sent them toppling. We wheeled around to aim another blast at the ground. More cracks spidered across the stone surface. A faint groaning reached my ears—the draugr, realizing they were doomed?

They'd been human once, but Surt had turned them

into monsters. I steeled myself for the next strike and the next, letting out a cheer as more of the dark rock crumbled down into the hollow depths beneath it. Loki motioned to us, and he and Baldur lashed out together, sending a flood of glittering flame through the caved in terrain. The few boulders that had been shifting went still, scorched black.

Just two more spots to hit—around the front, where the giants were roaring even louder now. We hadn't seen Surt yet, which seemed to show what Muninn had said was true. He wasn't here to rally his troops or to fight us off himself.

Surt's surface level guards were stepping one way and another, nearly colliding with each other, not sure which threat to deal with first. A growing horde of draugr shuffling up from the caves nearby milled around them. A few of the giants had managed to hurdle over the magma moat and were wrenching at the drawbridge. The creak of its hinges told me it wasn't going to hold much longer.

"Push them back, push them back!" Loki cried with a gleeful grin, pointing the guards toward the giants as if he and the other gods really were allied with Surt's side. The giants who spotted him let out bellows of rage. We didn't want to still be here when they broke through.

Thor shook his head at the trickster, but he was smiling too as he shouted for our next blast.

The ground gave way under the feet of the guards who'd been rushing at us. They and a bunch of the draugr above toppled down into the caverns. Other guards charged at us from the opposite direction, but

Freya and Tyr were there with their swords to fend them off. We hurled one last missile of power at the final spot the dark elves had marked for us.

A pit opened in the ground at the foot of the great tower of Surt, in the middle of his fortress. The tall structure teetered forward. My breath hitched as its front wall started to spill down into the pit like an architectural landslide.

Thor raised his hammer again, and I moved into battle position, even though I couldn't really help with this part. Another wave of flame crackled over and between the rubble.

We'd done it. We'd battered Surt's hall and torched his army.

Or had we? As I spun around, ready to find the gate to Asgard that must lie in the wreckage of that tower, a faint scraping sound reached my ears through the din. My gaze leapt to the cliff just behind the fortress walls.

There was an opening there. An opening that led to another cavern? The dark elves hadn't mentioned anywhere else Surt had stashed his undead soldiers, but they might not have known—or they might have been hedging their bets.

Loki darted over beside me. His ears, even sharper than mine, must have caught the noise too. "Burn and smash it?" he suggested.

"You read my mind," I said.

At his gesture, the others swept over the back wall with us. Loki led the attack this time. "Incinerate them!" he shouted with a slash of his hand, and we all launched ourselves at the cliff face as one.

A wave of fiery flickering light seared across the landscape and into the opening. Something hissed and crackled on the other side. From the swell of light, the flames had burst into an inferno within.

Thor had thrown his hammer at the same moment. It slammed into the cliff just above the entrance, and a real landslide poured down. With a thunder befitting the thunder god, a shower of boulders and smaller rocks piled over the opening.

"The gate," Baldur said, turning toward the ruin of the tower. "I can feel it—all of them. They're this way."

"We haven't dealt with Surt," Thor grumbled, smacking his hammer against his broad palm.

"That was the whole idea," Loki said. "We've devastated the army he spent decades building. We can hunt him down and skewer him in good time."

A giant's triumphant bellow and the crash of the drawbridge told us *we* might be skewered soon if we stuck around here any longer. "Come on," I said. "Let's go home."

26

Aria

Asgard really could be a lovely place when you weren't spending every spare moment preparing for a zombie invasion. I squirmed deeper into the soft grass, my head resting on Thor's thigh, my feet tucked under Baldur's arms where they were both sprawled in the field with me. A warm summer breeze drifted over us, and no sound interrupted my relaxation other than the chirping of a few birds gliding by.

Why had I ever found the idea of feeling this close to my gods scary? This was exactly where I was meant to be. I could feel *that* with every particle of my valkyrie being.

"Okay," I said. "It's decided. I think I'll just stay in this position forever."

Thor chuckled and brushed his hand over my hair. A short distance away, Loki perked up, shaking off his thoughtful reverie.

"But there are so many positions we haven't had the chance to try yet, pixie," he said in his smooth sly voice.

I rolled my eyes at him as well as I could while I was lying down. "Just let me enjoy the moment, okay?"

Soon, we were going to have to get back to work tracking down Surt. The war might be over, but there was nothing stopping the giant from gearing up for another attack while he was still on the loose. Baldur had suggested it might lighten all our spirits to take a day to recuperate before we started on that next quest, and I wasn't going to argue with that. Even if I wasn't sure my spirit could ever be totally "lightened" while the giant who'd meant to tear apart this world and my former one was still free somewhere, probably fuming at us.

A black form swooped by overhead—a bird that wasn't just a bird. Muninn had been reacquainting herself with Asgard, switching back and forth between her forms at random, as far as I could tell. She'd admitted to me this morning that she'd never experienced the realm of the gods as anything but a raven before now.

"You know what we could really use?" Hod said from his spot behind me. "Some of that fine mead, the kind we saved for the celebratory feasts."

Loki shot him an amused look. "You are not who I'd have expected to hear that suggestion from, Dark One."

"I can appreciate a good beverage," Hod said, matching Loki's playful tone. "Shouldn't you be able to figure out where we can get some, Sly One?"

Thor stirred. "We *do* have an excellent reason to celebrate."

I waved them all off. "You can have the mead. Just

bring me a beer while you're at it. Or a rum and Coke if that's on offer."

Baldur squeezed my foot affectionately. "You might not say that after you've tried proper Asgardian mead."

I grimaced. "After the amount of time I've spent in Valhalla in the last couple weeks, I think I've gotten my fill through osmosis. Don't you drink *anything* other than—"

A crackling sound broke through our banter. I stiffened, my head jerking up.

A torrent of fire was coursing against the sky, over the trees at the edge of the field.

My pulse hiccupped. I scrambled to my feet alongside the others. "Odin!" Tyr hollered.

The torrent arced and descended toward us, a bridge of flames. And standing at its crest was a burly man with a gray beard and a sword dancing with its own fire.

"Hello, Asgard," Surt roared. "I've finally come to finish what I started."

ABOUT THE AUTHOR

Eva Chase lives in Canada with her family. She loves stories both swoony and supernatural, and strong women and the men who appreciate them. Along with the Their Dark Valkyrie series, she is the author of the Witch's Consorts series, the Dragon Shifter's Mates series, the Demons of Fame Romance series, the Legends Reborn trilogy, and the Alpha Project Psychic Romance series.

Connect with Eva online:
www.evachase.com
eva@evachase.com

Printed in Great Britain
by Amazon

69009167R00149